# ENEMY COWBOY

## dobi daniels

Luxhaven
Publishing

ISBN paperback, 978-1-958987-15-5


Interior Design by Luxhaven Publishing

Cover Design by The Book Brander Boutique

Editing by JD Book Services

Proofreading by Lisa Lee Proofreading

*To JC, Grandma D, and DC, whom I love more than life itself.*

**A Cowboy Loves the Doctor Series**

A Doctor Second Chance for the Rancher (prequel)

A Doctor Blind Date for the Cowboy

A Doctor Enemy for the Cowboy

A Doctor Billionaire for the Cowboy

**Dexington Doctor Billionaires Series**

Loving The Billionaire Heir Doc

Loving The Billionaire Owner Doc

Loving The Billionaire Army Doc

Loving The Billionaire Cowboy Doc

Loving The Billionaire Boss Doc

**Dexington Christmas Billionaires Series**

A Billionaire Inventor for Christmas

A Billionaire Butler for Christmas

A Billionaire Dentist for Christmas

**Standalone**

Her Billionaire Nemesis (short story)

# SEE ALL OF DOBI DANIELS BOOKS

at https://dobidaniels.com

# AUTHOR'S NOTE

Thank you for choosing A DOCTOR ENEMY FOR THE COWBOY. I enjoyed writing the story of Tara Ellis and Rex Dexin, two very emotional characters!

Sometimes it's hard to ask for and accept forgiveness, or to feel you don't deserve love because of your choices, some of which may have been beyond your control. I pray A DOCTOR ENEMY FOR THE COWBOY gives you hope to believe there's someone who'd love you just the way you are, and that love is still possible for you no matter what.

Please continue this journey with me in A DOCTOR BILLIONAIRE FOR THE COWBOY, which is the story of how Rex's brother, Jax, found love. You can grab your copy at https://dobidaniels.com.

Would you like to be notified when the next Dobi Daniels book releases? Sign up at https://dobidaniels.com.

Once again, thank you so much for purchasing A DOCTOR ENEMY FOR THE COWBOY and for meeting Tara Ellis and Rex Dexin. If you enjoyed it, please consider leaving a review at your favorite retailer or recommending it to a friend.

Thanks again for your support!

Dobi Daniels

# A Doctor ENEMY for the COWBOY

"Hey! Leave her alone!" Rex Dexin steeled himself as the group of boys surrounding the scrawny girl with blonde pigtails turned as one in his direction. Rex was supposed to meet his friends at Grandma Dee's corner store on Main Street. The little shop had all kinds of flavors of popsicles, cold and perfect for the hot summer afternoon, but it seemed he'd arrived before the others. And even though he didn't recognize the girl standing next to the beaten-up pickup truck, he knew the boys all too well.

*Oscar and his little bullies.* That was the name he'd coined for these classmates, who all seemed to hunt for trouble like a dog after bone. And even though the little brat, Oscar, was only in fifth grade like him, he already had the makings of a thug-in-training. People said Oscar had become that way because his ma had left his pa for some two-bit ranch hand who came through town, but Rex knew better—Oscar had always loved holding power over others he thought weaker than himself. He'd even ripped Melissa's poster—poor girl—when she'd come to class with it for show-and-tell, and Oscar had realized it was bigger than everyone else's, even his.

Rex tried to ignore him for the most part, since he didn't like getting into fights, but harassing a girl was a line Oscar wasn't supposed to cross. Ma had taught him girls needed to be protected.

He planted his feet firmly on the ground and squared his shoulders. "I said leave her alone," Rex repeated.

The boys looked at one another and then back at Oscar as if waiting for his signal. But Rex wasn't worried—Oscar knew better than to try to fight him; the last time he'd done it, Oscar had ended up at the dentist's. Rex hated violence, but he disliked a bully more.

"No need to get all twisted up," Oscar said as he raised his hands in mock surrender. "We were just having a chat with the little lady."

Rex scoffed. *Little lady*. Did Oscar think he was

The Godfather? The movie had been all the rave in town a few months ago, but Rex hadn't cared for it. Too many killings if you asked him.

"Well, the talk is over," Rex said, keeping his eyes steady on Oscar.

"Okay, okay," Oscar said. "Let's go, boys."

They marched past Rex and behind Oscar like little ants and soon disappeared at the end of the street.

Rex's shoulders relaxed. Even though he could take on Oscar one-on-one, it wouldn't have been a smart idea to fight the whole group.

"I can take care of myself just fine," the girl said, her chin up and her eyes blazing in anger.

The girl had spunk for sure. But why was she treating him like enemy when he'd only helped her? "Sure," he replied, though he didn't think she'd have been able to handle Oscar and his cronies.

He moved over and leaned against the crates beside the store's entrance, which gave him a better view of the girl, who seemed to be clutching a small book against her chest. The girl looked rather small for her age, with her hair braided into untidy pigtails and her worn jeans barely reaching her ankles. But he guessed she must be only a year or two younger than himself.

Rex frowned. Where was her family, and why was she here alone?

He looked through the store windows and noticed a man in a striped T-shirt and black corduroy pants at the checkout counter. Maybe that was her father. Then he turned back to her only to find her eyes on him.

Rex stared back. The girl wasn't pretty like his classmate Darla—Darla had even won a spot on a national milk commercial, and all the boys liked her. Well, except for him of course. Rex wasn't interested in girls. Give him a horse and an old vintage car any day and he was happy.

But there was something about this girl's large brown eyes he couldn't look away from. He adjusted the cowboy hat on his head. "What's that?" he asked, gesturing at the book she held.

"*Oliver Twist*."

*Surprise, surprise*. Who would have thought? Maggie, his ma's friend, had been on his case about reading books that weren't about horses and had given him the same book to read. It wasn't common reading material in these parts, and he'd found it interesting. "Good book," he said.

"You've read it?" she asked in a voice that indicated she didn't believe him.

"Yes. I want some more."

She laughed, a sweet sound that made his heart feel funny. Rex wished he could hear it again.

"Thank you for your help," she finally said.

"Anytime," he replied. "I'll always protect you."

Rex's face turned red. Now why did he go and say that? He didn't really know her, and now she'd think he was a creep.

"Thanks for saying that," she replied softly with a smile.

Something in his chest expanded at her words, and suddenly, Rex realized he wanted her to believe it. "I mean it."

"Okay, Oliver Twist," she said. Rex could see she was fighting back another smile.

"That's not my name."

"I know. But I like it," she said. "I'm Rose by the way."

Rex's eyebrows rose. "You don't look like my aunt." Rose was the name of *Oliver Twist*'s maternal aunt.

Rose chuckled, the sound warming his insides. Now he wanted to see her smile again. "Red or white?" he asked.

She laughed, a clear pure sound he wished could

go on and on. "White. Mama said it stands for innocence."

Innocent Rose. He liked that. "It's a beautiful name." And she must have liked what he said, because her face turned all pink and she smiled again.

Rex's ears grew warm for some reason, so he changed the topic. "You live with your ma?" he asked.

Her face fell. "She's in heaven."

Rex cursed himself for taking the smile away. "I'm sorry."

"It's not your fault."

"So you live around here?" Rex had never seen her before, but that didn't mean anything. She could just be new to the area, though he doubted it, since most of the families here were either ranchers or farmers, and the girl and the man in the store didn't strike him as one of either.

She shook her head. "From New York."

Rex had heard about the place only because they had classic car shows there. He'd never been, but the city didn't interest him—Rex liked it just fine on his ranch with his horses. "So just passing through."

"Sort of," she replied.

A familiar jingle pierced the air, and Rex guessed her father was on his way out of the store.

Rose must have realized it too, because her face turned serious. "Can I write you?" she asked.

No one had made this request of Rex before, but something in her voice told him she yearned for a friend. Yet if she sent a letter to the ranch where he lived, he'd never hear the end of it from his two brothers. Somehow he wanted this letter to be private, and Paul, the corner store owner, would make sure Rex received it—he was nice like that to all the kids.

"Sure," he said. "You can send the letter to this store."

"Rose, get in the truck!" a gravelly voice barked. Rose flinched.

Rex could feel his temper rising. No girl deserved to be spoken to like that, by her father or by anyone else. It was obvious the man didn't care much about her. He turned to the man in question. Despite some resemblance to Rose like he'd expected, something about the man's surly face struck Rex as wrong.

He glanced at Rose and saw the subtle shake of her head. She didn't want him to interfere. So as much as Rex would have loved to bite off the man's head, he held himself back for her sake.

Her father strode over to the driver's side of the truck, jerked the door open, and jumped in. Rose scrambled to enter the truck on the passenger side. As he started the engine, the sound of which made Rex think it was probably on its last legs, Rose placed the book against the window and pointed at it.

*Oliver Twist*. The nickname she'd chosen for him.

As the truck sped off leaving dust in its wake, Rex understood what she'd been trying to say.

She would write to him. A letter just for him.

And Rex decided he'd wait for her letter, no matter how long it took. He'd tell Paul to watch out for it.

Rex would be her Oliver Twist.

# CHAPTER 2

## SEVENTEEN YEARS AGO

Rose Tara Ellis hurriedly stuffed her most precious belongings in her backpack and glanced around the room she shared with her roommate Catherine to see if she'd missed anything. She had to leave now if she wanted to escape.

Rose had been ecstatic when she'd gained admission into one of the most prestigious high school academies in upstate New York. She might have been poor—which wasn't helped by the fact that her father drank away his wages more than half the time—but Rose had always known her book smarts were the ticket out of the hellhole she'd grown up in, so she'd put in the work.

And it had paid off.

She'd received a full scholarship to the academy. And even though she was the known charity case in her class, Rose had managed to remain inconspicuous, and her freshman year as well as the fall semester of her sophomore year at the boarding school had been relatively uneventful. She'd ignored everything else and focused on her studies. She'd even become close friends with her roommate Catherine. Catherine came from a modest family, but she'd never looked down on Rose.

But then Rose had caught the eye of William Carriford, the number one playboy at the academy.

She'd been aware of his reputation and had done her best to avoid him and his group of hangers-on. His parents were said to be the richest in the school, and his mother was on the board of directors. William believed he was entitled to whatever he wanted.

And he wanted Rose.

But Rose wasn't for the taking, and thankfully she'd managed to dodge him for most of the spring term. Because of the term paper she'd submitted for her World History class instead of a written exam, Rose had completed her schoolwork for the semester and could leave the campus ahead of everyone else. She'd had no plans to stay back for the week-long activities that typically followed the end of exams before the school closed for the summer break, but she'd miss saying goodbye to Catherine before leaving. Rose resolved to make it up to her another time.

She stuffed her coin purse in her jeans pocket, her wallet in the front zipper of her backpack, and strapped the bag on. Then she flung the door open to leave.

"Hello, beautiful," a voice drawled.

Rose's eyes widened, but she managed to tamp down her trepidation. William's sidekicks—she thought of them as Dumb One and Dumb Two—were standing outside her door as if waiting for her. How had they known she'd be leaving now? Rose hadn't told anyone her plan. And how did they get in? The girls' dorm was off-limits to the boys except for the general reception room.

She straightened her shoulders. She would not show any fear to these bullies. "What do you want?" Rose asked in a tight voice.

"William wants to see you," Dumb Two replied, tweaking his patrician nose, which was a bit too large for his face. Both guys played high school football and were built like linebackers. Rose had a feeling they might have used some "juice" to bulk up.

"Why?" she asked flatly.

"I don't know. I'm only the messenger."

"I'll come by and see him later," Rose said.

Dumb One shook his head, his perfectly tousled brown hair hardly moving. "That won't work. You know he hates waiting."

"I'll hold this for you like a gentleman," Dumb Two said. He grabbed her backpack before she could resist and tossed it over his shoulder.

Rose scoffed. *Gentleman indeed.* More like he didn't want to give her a chance to run away. As her mind scrambled to figure a way out, Dumb One grabbed her arm and dragged her after him with Dumb Two attached on her other side.

They led her down the dorm's hallway. Fortunately, most students were still taking their final exams, otherwise the news about her personal escort service would be all over the school already. Did it mean these two dumbos hadn't bothered with the exams?

Soon they were outside, and the guys led her in the direction of a red-bricked edifice set apart from other nearby buildings that had been arranged in an oval pattern around a central courtyard. It was rumored only a very select group of students got to live in the red building, which consisted of apartments instead of dorm rooms, perfect for all the weekly parties the privileged students held. Rose had also heard the horror stories of what happened there, but somehow nothing ever happened to the perpetrators. Most students were willing to give an arm or a leg for an invite to one such event, yet Rose had never been interested—licking people's boots was not her thing, and she'd never fit in anyway. She was only at the school to get the education needed to guarantee her a spot to her Ivy League school of choice, nothing more.

Rose's mind spun as they passed through the courtyard and neared the building. She had to escape. It was now or never.

She stumbled and crashed to the ground, Dumb One's grip on her falling off. "Ouch!" she said as she rubbed her knee, her face scrunched up in pain.

"What is it?" Dumb One said with a look of impatience.

"I just tripped on my shoelace," Rose said. "Give me a minute to fix it."

"Alright, but hurry up," Dumb Two said in annoyance.

Rose pretended to retie the laces of her sneakers. But then she suddenly sprang up and sprinted away. It meant leaving her backpack behind, but what could she do? Entering that building was tantamount to signing her death warrant.

"Stop!" Dumb One screamed as both boys realized what had happened and ran after her.

But Rose didn't halt. Instead she increased her speed and soon exited the courtyard, zigzagging between the buildings before dropping out of view behind one of them.

She poked out her head to scan the area. Dumb One and Dumb Two stood at one end of the courtyard, their eyes searching for her. Rose ducked her head as their eyes flicked in her direction. Hopefully, they hadn't seen her. She let out an exhale when she was sure there were no footsteps headed her way. But Rose had to leave this spot soon if she wanted to stay safe. She needed to come up with a plan.

Buying a train ticket to leave town was not an option—Dumb Two still had her bag, which held her wallet. She had no close friends she could run to and ask for money except Catherine, but going back to the dorm to find her was out of the question. It was the first place the guys would look for her.

Then she remembered the coin purse and patted her jean pocket. Thank goodness it was still intact. The coins in it were enough to call her father. Rose usually returned home on her own for school breaks, but this was an emergency. Her father had been doing better these days instead of drowning himself in an alcoholic stupor with whatever little earnings he had, and he'd even gotten his job back at the plant. He'd managed to send some money to her during the semester for the first time, which had supplemented the cash she'd saved from the odd jobs she worked during her school breaks.

Rose's father had lost interest in everything around him, including Rose, after her mom died. He'd stopped caring, and Rose had only managed to keep food on the table with the part-time work she'd done for their neighbor, Miss Whitaker. She'd cooked meals, done the dishes, washed the laundry, and cleaned the house for the elderly lady all through middle school until she'd gotten her admission at the academy. Miss Whitaker had been a life saver, but sometimes she was so out of it. She'd often mistake Rose for her dead daughter, and one time she'd even told Rose she thought she'd died. But Rose had enjoyed working for her, and the times she spent in the woman's home gave her some much-needed breathing room from her father.

But she needed him now. Rose had to call him and then find a place to hide until he arrived, and she knew where she could achieve both goals.

Casting one more look in the direction of the courtyard to make sure Dumb One and Dumb Two were still there, Rose snuck behind the school buildings until she managed to reach the southern side of the campus. Then she arrived at her destination.

The old barn on the school property had been abandoned for a while before it had been converted into a space for storing cleaning supplies. Rose had become good friends with the old school janitor, Mr. Rushfield, after she'd helped him right his cart when one of the students had flipped it over as a prank. So when she'd bemoaned her need for a quiet place to study when all the spots in the library were taken, he'd shown her the barn—which was empty most of the time—and had even given her a spare key to the place. Rose had spent many quiet evenings studying there. Mr. Rushfield had also permitted her to use the lone phone in the place in case of an emergency.

Like now.

Luckily, her ring of keys was in her back pocket. Rose pulled them out and unlocked the barn before slipping in and shutting it behind her, obliterating the evening light that had illuminated the space.

Her shoulders relaxed. She was safe for now. Though it was somewhat dark, Rose was familiar enough with the large, cavernous space and soon hurried through, leaving dust in her wake. She reached the office in the back and entered. Various cleaning items were stored in one corner of the room, while a cushioned chair and a desk occupied another. A coin-operated pay phone hung on the wall above the desk. The school maintained a couple of these phones around the premises but usually in locations under supervision. Rose was fortunate this one wasn't one of them.

She fished out her coin purse, extracted the coins she needed, and dialed her home phone number. The phone rang a couple times, and then the line connected.

"Hello?" a rough voice said.

Rose froze when she recognized the voice. Matt, her father's so-called friend—the heavyset man who'd always stared at her with a lewd smile. Matt had grabbed her backside once when her father wasn't looking, and when Rose had told her father about it, he'd insisted it was just her imagination. Still, he'd agreed to never bring Matt over to the house.

But it seemed her father had broken his promise.

Rose felt disappointment wash over her. Why couldn't her father keep his word to her for once? It was almost like she had no place in his life. Yet she swallowed the bitterness that threatened to rise in her, since she still needed him.

"Can I speak to my father?" she asked in an emotionless voice.

"Ah, sweet, sweet Rose." She hated the way Matt called her name. "You want to talk to your father? Then you have to be nice to me."

"Who is it?" Rose heard a drunken voice call out in the background before letting out a loud belch.

Her heart sank. Her father had fallen off the wagon and started drinking again, even though he'd promised her he'd stay sober.

"Just some salesperson," Matt replied.

"Oh, screw those guys," her father said. Glass crashed on the floor as he tried to move. "I need more beer."

"Coming right up," Matt said. "Rose, you sweet thing, when are you coming back?"

Rose slammed the receiver into its cradle and leaned against the wall for support as tears filled her eyes. How could her father fail her yet again? Even if he'd picked up the phone, he was no help to her in his drunken state, and going home now would mean trouble with Matt there. This sucked big time.

She took a deep breath. Rose still had to save herself, even if her father couldn't. But who could she call? She was an only child and had no other relatives. She also had no friends back home—her father's alcoholism had isolated her in the town she grew up in. And there was no way Miss Whitaker could help. So who could she reach out to?

Then she remembered him.

*I'll always protect you,* his words echoed.

He'd said the words the first time he'd met her, but soon the phrase had become their fond way of signing off each note to each other. Rose had found the corner store's address and phone number in the business directory her father liked to pick up as a souvenir in any town he'd visited—it was a strange habit he'd had for years, but Rose had never been more grateful for it than at the time.

The name Oliver Twist had stuck, and it made everything between them seem like a fairytale. They'd started off sharing the books they'd read and loved, but soon their letters became more personal, and eventually they were telling each other things they'd told no one else.

Oliver wanted to become a horse breeder, but raising horses was prohibitively expensive, so he'd been working a lot after school and saving for it. He'd even gotten a part-time job at the corner store, which made it easier for them to write to each other.

Rose, on the other hand, wanted to become a pediatrician—she'd liked children since she was young, and Mama had always said she was good with them. But they never talked about their families. It was like they wanted no intrusion of their real life on what they had. And then their letter exchange had slowed as Rose started at the academy.

But now her real life had come knocking, and Rose needed Oliver.

With the words *I'll always protect you* echoing in her ears, Rose took a deep breath, dropped in another set of coins, and dialed the number from memory.

The line rang once and then connected. "Good evening. Thank you for calling Grandma Dee's retail store," a young male's warm voice drawled. "How may I help you?"

"May I speak with Oliver?"

There was a sharp intake of breath on the other end of the line. "Rose?"

It was as if she'd been desperate for air and suddenly got a lungful of it. "Oliver."

He chuckled as if he couldn't believe it. "It's really you." Then as if he'd sensed something over the line, "Is everything alright?"

"Can you come pick me up?"

"Where do I need to go?" he asked simply.

Rose choked back a sob. He hadn't questioned. She was sure he'd have plans for the evening. But Oliver was coming, just because she'd asked. "I'm at school." Rose had shared the good news with him when she'd gotten her admission, and she repeated the address to him.

"I'm leaving right now and should be there in a few hours," he said. "I'll ask for you at the school gate once I get there, and I'll be wearing a red checkered shirt over jeans. Are you in a safe place?"

"Yes."

"Okay. Stay there. Everything is going to be alright, Rose."

"Thank you."

"That's what friends are for. I'll see you soon."

"Bye." She placed the receiver back in its cradle and slumped into the chair, resting her head on the desk.

Rose felt the fear in her heart unfurl and slither away.

She was going to be alright.

Because her Oliver was on his way to protect her like he'd promised.

Rex dropped the phone in its receiver, folded up the piece of paper on which he'd written the address, and grabbed his jacket from where it hung on the wall behind him.

"Is everything alright?" Paul, the owner of the corner store where Rex worked part-time, asked with a frown on his face as he watched Rex zip up his jacket in a hurry.

"Do you mind if I leave now?" Rex asked. "I promise I'll make it up to you next week."

"That's not a problem. What's going on?"

It was a good thing he'd been working today at the corner store, otherwise he would have missed Rose's call. "It's Rose. She's in trouble and needs my help."

"Your friend, Rose? The one in New York?" Paul knew all about the letters.

"Yes. I need to head up to New York to pick her up." They'd only exchanged letters all these years, but Rose had been calm in the face of bullies when he'd met her for the first time, so hearing her sound so frazzled had him very worried. He figured she must have gotten the store's phone number the same way she'd gotten the address. He needed to hurry home to pick up one of their ranch's trucks, even though it would mean losing precious time, time he needed to get to Rose as fast as possible. Rex had gotten his driver's license last year, though he'd been driving vehicles on their large property for much longer than that.

"Here, take my car keys," Paul said.

"Are you sure?" Rex asked.

Paul waved his concern away. "Taking it would be easier for you, and the gas tank is full. Don't worry, I'll call my wife to pick me up." He opened the money box and pulled out a bunch of notes. "Here. Take this as well."

"I can't accept that."

"Take it in case your friend needs it. You can always pay me back later."

Rex accepted the keys and the money. "Thank you." The car would definitely help him in getting to New York faster, and though he already had enough money on him, the extra cash might come in handy.

Rex rushed out of the store into the cool evening fall air and hurried over to the Ford pickup truck parked on the curb. He slid in, started the vehicle, and drove it down Main Street until he connected to a narrow road that led to the highway.

He forced his mind to stay calm. Something terrible must have happened to Rose for her to run away from school and not go home. Rex would have to take her to his house, and she'd meet his family, which meant he'd have to figure out what to tell them about her. But he didn't care about the fallout from that as long as Rose arrived safe and sound. Rex was certain his mom would extend the courteous western hospitality the Dexins were known for to her no matter what.

As he drove along the narrow, deserted road, Rex slowed down, though it was hard to resist the urge to go over the speed limit and hurry to Rose as fast as he could. The sky had darkened, and it was becoming hard to see what was ahead of him. This area of the road had been under construction during the last few weeks, and there'd been quite a few accidents on it, but mostly from out-of-town visitors who didn't seem to care about the caution signs visible along the way. Rex needed to be careful, but hopefully, he'd be off this stretch of road in a few minutes.

He spotted an intersection coming up ahead, and he let out a sigh of relief. Soon he'd be at the turn-off that led to the highway. The overhead traffic light turned green just as he reached the intersection, and Rex raced through, intent on reaching the turn-off as fast as he could.

Twin lights blinded him from the right, and a

heavy truck rammed into the passenger side of Rex's truck.

The window shattered, raining glass on Rex even as his body hit the steering wheel. But the restraining seatbelt jerked him back as he fought to regain control of the pickup, the sounds of screeching brakes, bending metal, and tires skidding on the asphalt filling the air.

But it was no use.

The pickup spun as the heavy truck hit Rex's vehicle a second time. His head crashed against the steering wheel, and his body jolted as it received the second blow, the weight pressing down on him even as glass from the blown-out windshield cascaded all over him.

Rex's vision distorted as he went in and out of consciousness.

Then everything went black.

Rose released the latch on the barn door, pushed one of the doors open, and peered outside. The night sky had darkened, but she could make out no one in the immediate area. Oliver would have arrived at the school gates by now, and Rose needed to go to him, since no one knew she'd holed up in the barn.

She stepped out, locked the barn, and inhaled the cool spring air before striding down the path that led in the direction of the school's entrance. Soon she arrived near the school gates and hid behind the flower hedges that lined the cobblestone road running from the door of the school's main administrative building, taking care to avoid the security guards. Luckily, it seemed they'd confined themselves to the gatehouse.

Rose looked beyond the gates to the parking lot outside. There was no tall young man wearing a red checkered shirt waiting there. Did it mean Oliver hadn't arrived?

She checked the time on her watch, a cheap but sturdy second-hand piece she'd bought with the money she'd made on her last summer job, and frowned. It was way past the expected time for him to arrive. Had something happened to him? No! She couldn't afford to think bad thoughts. He had to be alright and on his way, because Oliver would never leave her stranded here—he'd always struck her as a person of his word. She would wait as long as it took.

Rose adjusted her position to make herself more comfortable and settled in to watch out for him. Soon the air grew cooler, and she wrapped her arms around herself to ward off the cold. A few cars came and went, but none of the occupants resembled Oliver. Eventually, the security guards locked down the gates for the night.

Yet there was no Oliver.

Disappointment welled up in her. What had happened? But Rose couldn't stay where she was any longer. Her best option was to return to the barn and then figure out what to do next. In the worst-case scenario, she could spend the night there and maybe borrow some money for the train ticket from Mr. Rushfield when he arrived for work in the morning. Rose was sure William Carriford was still hunting for her. He wasn't the type to give up when he'd set his sights on his next conquest. So returning to the dorm was not an option.

Rose moved away from the flower hedges and was soon back on the path that led to the barn. She arrived at the building, pulled out her keys, and reached for the lock.

"Well, well, well. It's about time."

Rose spun to see William Carriford standing there with his sidekicks flanking him. How had they found her?

"I can't believe she was here, just like Catherine said she would be," Dumb Two said with a chuckle.

Rose felt cold wash over her. So Catherine, her so-called best friend, had betrayed her. Rose had mentioned the place to her once when Catherine had looked all over campus for her, wanting to borrow her class notes for an upcoming test. And now, she'd divulged the information to William, even though she was aware of what he was capable of.

But Rose had to get out of here. As if anticipating her thoughts, Dumb One and Two had blocked all possible exit routes. Rose's mind raced. Her only option was to make it into the barn and lock herself inside. The lock was solid enough that any attempt by William and his group to break it down would create enough of a ruckus to bring the security guards running.

Rose stood a step back until her back was against the barn door. Then she reached for the lock behind her. She needed a few minutes to open it, so she had to keep William talking until then.

"What do you want, William?" she asked even as she struggled to slip the key into the lock's opening.

Her heart thundered as he walked toward her. "You know what I want."

"I don't," Rose replied, keeping her voice steady even as she twisted the key in the lock.

The lock popped open.

Rose winced at the faint sound. Had they heard it too? She wasn't sure, but she couldn't stop now. All she needed to do now was unhook the lock, push the barn door open, and then she would be in.

"You can't run away from me, Rose," William said as he stopped a few feet away from her. "Not now, not ever."

Her hands shook as she unhooked the lock as slowly as she could. "I don't belong to you," she said. Just a few more seconds, and she would be out of harm's way.

William shook his head as if scolding an errant child. "Everything in this school belongs to me, and that includes you." In an unexpected move, he surged toward her.

Rose shoved the barn door open, rushed in, and then tried to slam the door shut.

But she was no match for William and his goons and was soon thrown back against the floor.

William reached her and grabbed her hair, pulling her further into the barn.

"Let me go," Rose cried and swung her free hand

at his face. It connected with his jaw, and she felt pain radiate down her arm.

William grimaced with pain, losing his hold on her. Rose spun away and raced toward the entrance of the barn. Her sanctuary was no longer safe.

But he soon caught her waist from behind and clamped his hand down hard on her mouth as he pulled her back into the barn. "You think you can hide from me?" he said with a vicious jerk of her hair.

Rose felt fear rising within her, but she shoved it down. She had an idea of what he was about to do, and she couldn't let it happen. So Rose fought William with everything in her and bit the palm that covered her mouth.

"Aargh!" William said and swung a blow at her head.

Pain exploded in Rose's head, and her vision dimmed. She slumped against him, desperately trying to clear her head.

"I'll show you what happens to those who play games with me," William promised in a menacing tone.

Rose wasn't sure if her jaw was broken, but she could feel her cheek swelling, and her voice barely came out as a squeak when she tried to cry out for help.

But no one came to save her. Why had she deceived herself into thinking that anyone, including Oliver, cared for her?

Rose curled into a ball to protect herself as much as she could even as her vision dimmed.

Then the lights went out.

# CHAPTER 3

## SEVENTEEN YEARS AGO

"Is he going to be alright?" Rex heard his ma's sweet voice ask as if from afar. His eyes refused to open, and everywhere on his body hurt, especially his left leg. Rex couldn't even tell where he was.

"Yes," a familiar voice said. It sounded like Dr. Brennan, their family doctor, which meant Rex was either at the ranch or in the hospital at Dexington where Dr. Brennan worked. "Fortunately, he came away with no major damage except for a mild concussion, a hairline fracture of his tibia, and extensive bruises. But we need to observe him for a while to make sure there's no further head injury. Rex won't need surgery for the leg, but he'll need to wear a brace for some time and get enough rest to let the bone heal well."

"Thank you, Doctor. I'll make sure he gets the rest he needs," his ma said, the relief evident in her voice. "What about the other driver?"

"He made it out alive. Turns out he had a faulty brake that caused the accident."

Rex remembered the bone-crushing sound that had filled the air as a truck rammed into his vehicle.

But he was forgetting something... something really important.

Rex's breath quickened. What was it? *Think, Rex.* His mind seemed clouded, as if there were holes in his memory he couldn't fill.

"When will he wake up?" Ma asked.

"We gave him something for the pain, so I expect in a few hours. But he needs all the sleep he can get now," Dr. Brennan replied.

Rex's heart raced. He had to remember. Something... someone. But who?

Then a name came to him: Rose.

But it was too late.

Rex was powerless to resist as he slipped away into unconsciousness.

~

"Hello, can you hear me?"

Rose struggled to open her eyes, and her vision wavered. Her head ached like a hammer had been taken to it, and everywhere else hurt so bad. Finally, her vision cleared, and she saw a dark-skinned middle-aged woman with warm eyes in a white uniform hovering over her. Rose tried to sit up, but her body refused to cooperate, and she collapsed back on the white sheets. Where was she?

"It's okay," the nurse said. "You're in the hospital a county over from your school. You're safe now."

Safe? Then the memory of the assault came roaring back at her, and Rose let out a whimper.

"Shh. You're going to be alright," the nurse said as she sat on the hospital bed beside Rose and wiped away the tears that had trickled down Rose's cheeks.

Rose tried to turn away—she didn't need anybody's sympathy.

That was when she felt the pain, the one deep and aching in her pelvis, like her insides had been shredded into pieces.

And in that moment, she realized the truth, and a sob choked out of her.

What she'd been running from had finally happened to her.

William had hurt her, really hurt her, and stolen

something Rose would never get back again.

The nurse gathered Rose tenderly in her arms as if she knew what was on Rose's mind. "You'll be alright, dear," she said. "You can let it all out."

It was as if she was in her mama's arms again, and Rose couldn't hold back the sobs.

Why had this happened to her? She didn't deserve any of it.

Rose felt like crushing everything around her. She wanted someone else to feel the pain that was tearing her up from the inside out. But instead, all she could do was cry until it felt like her soul had emptied out. Soon her sobs turned to sniffles.

"We'll catch the bastard that did this to you," the nurse said.

But Rose knew who'd done it. She didn't believe anything would come of it, though she was grateful for the nurse's words. It comforted her to know someone, even a stranger, was in her corner.

There was a knock on the hospital room door, but Rose didn't look up.

"I'll be right back," the nurse said and released Rose.

Rose curled into herself as she laid back on the hospital bed. Soon the nurse returned and touched Rose's arm. Rose turned to look at her.

"The police would like to speak with you."

But Rose didn't want to meet them. She didn't want to see anyone. She wanted everyone to just go away and leave her alone.

The nurse patted her arm as if sensing her anxiety. "They'll need your help in catching the person that did this. Don't worry, dear. I'll be right here with you."

But it was only going to be a fruitless exercise. If nothing else, Rose knew the way the world treated the weak.

Justice in this case wasn't going to be served.

Three weeks later, Rex stood holding a crutch in front of the blue- and white-shuttered house that was Rose's address from the letters he'd received over the years. Once he'd regained full consciousness, Rex had been forced to stay on full bed rest by his ma. But he'd gotten the number Rose had called him on from Paul and called, yet there'd been no response. He'd also called the school, but at the mention of Rose's name, the person on the other end of the line had stated there was no Rose at the academy and cut off the call. His subsequent calls had been ignored.

Rex had written next, but Rose never replied. Scared out of his mind for her, Rex had finally convinced his ma to let him out of the house and had gotten his brother, Max, to drive him all the way to New York. Rex needed to see for himself that Rose was fine.

But the house appeared deserted.

"She's dead," a frail voice said loudly. Rex turned to see an elderly woman with white hair pulled up into a bun, leaning on a cane as she stood in the next-door neighbor's driveway.

Rex staggered, but his brother steadied him. Dead? It couldn't be true. The woman had to be talking about someone else—not Rose. "Good evening, ma'am," he said. "Do you mean Rose?"

The woman nodded. "Very nice girl too. She used to help me a lot around the house. I always teased her about her hair. You know, all that blonde with the red in it. Overheard the father saying the poor thing had been attacked outside the school gates. And now she's dead."

The truth slammed into Rex like a brick, and he gasped. The school gates. The place where Rex was supposed to meet her. Instead, he'd failed her.

Something wilted within Rex. Rose was dead, and it was all because of him. If only he'd arrived to get her like he'd promised. It was all his fault, and now it was too late.

"What about her father?" Max asked. Rex had told him Rose lived with her pa.

"Her father up and left one night," the old lady said. "Haven't seen him since."

Rex didn't care about him—the man had failed to protect Rose too. "Do you know where she's buried?" Rex asked instead. He had to see her one more time.

The woman shook her head. "No idea. So sad. She was just a pretty little thing too. Had big dreams to become a doctor."

Yes, that was his Rose. And now she was gone.

"Rex, are you alright?" Max asked.

Rex took a deep breath and let it out. He didn't know the answer to that.

And he wasn't even sure if he'd ever be okay again.

Rose stared out the large hospital window. Spring had made way for summer, and now the flowers were in full bloom and the leaves on the trees had turned green and vibrant. Even the birds chirped loudly as they flitted from tree to tree. But Rose felt none of their joy. She crushed the paper in her hand.

In the three weeks since the incident had happened, her life had turned upside down. Though a rape kit had pinned William as the assailant, he hadn't been charged—his family's power and money had buried the case without further investigation. Instead, the family's lawyer had tried to offer her money to disappear, but Rose had shoved the money in his face and told him to get out and never return. She wanted nothing to do with them.

But it seemed the family had felt slighted by her rejection. Rose had received a letter from the school saying she'd been expelled for conduct unbecoming of a student, though they were happy to give her recommendations to any other school she wanted to go to. She hadn't known whether to laugh or cry at the irony.

Her father had appeared, looking all remorseful, but Rose had refused to meet his gaze—nothing he could say could make up for his failure, and she was tired of all the disappointments and excuses. She'd eventually forgive him, but that didn't mean she was ready to go back to the way things had been.

The doctors had insisted she remain longer at the hospital to heal fully, but Rose had been worried about the mounting hospital bills. However, Miss Hyacinth, the kind nurse who'd stayed by her side, assured her the expenses had been covered by one of the hospital's anonymous funds. Her father had also chosen to be with her instead of going home, but Rose paid him no mind.

Even though her life was in pieces, Rose had figured she could start all over again.

Then she'd missed her period.

Rose had confided in Miss Hyacinth, who'd said it was probably due to the trauma she'd gone through, but she'd also insisted on a blood test—the result of which Rose now held in her hand. Her heart had shattered as she'd read the contents.

She was pregnant with the rapist's baby.

How could her life have gotten any worse? What was she going to do now?

Rose's heart raced. She trembled as her throat tightened, and suddenly she felt as if she was losing control.

Then Miss Hyacinth, who'd brought the result, placed a hand on Rose's shoulder. "Take a deep breath, honey, and let it out," she said. "Yes, that's it. Now do it again."

Rose repeated the exercise until she felt her heart slow down, back to its normal pace.

Miss Hyacinth patted her shoulder. "You're going to be just fine." And something about the way she'd said it made Rose believe her.

"I can't go back home," Rose whispered to her, but she was certain her father heard her words from where he leaned against the wall. Her life back in her town had already been unbearable. With the news of what had happened to her? It would be utterly miserable and would break her. She didn't need that now, not when she had to be stronger than ever.

"Mr. Ellis, would you mind if Rose stayed with me at my home?" Miss Hyacinth asked her father. "I can take good care of her there for as long as both you and she want."

Rose's eyes widened as she stared at Miss Hyacinth. She'd totally not expected the offer.

"I have a big enough place my husband left for me after he died," Miss Hyacinth continued. "And I live there all alone. Taking care of Rose would be a pleasure for me. You can come and have a look to make sure it's safe for her if you like, and you'll always be welcomed to see her at any time."

Rose didn't know what to say. For some reason, her heart warmed to the idea, though Miss Hyacinth was practically a stranger. But she'd only ever heard the other medical staff sing her praises. Besides, Rose would find a way to make her own money so as not to be a burden to her.

She looked at her father. He must have read something in her eyes, because he nodded slightly before turning to the nurse. "I'd like that," he said.

Miss Hyacinth beamed a large smile. "Great! I'll make all the arrangements and let you know."

Rose's shoulders relaxed, but then she remembered the result in her hand, and her fist tightened.

It was the worst news ever, the last thing she needed in her already devastated life.

But she was going to survive this. She had to.

Even though Oliver and her father had failed her, she would not fail herself.

She would rise from the ashes. She would reinvent herself if that was what it took to make a fresh start.

But she would no longer be a rose. Even though a rose had thorns, it was still delicate and could be hurt. Instead, she would be Tara, a tower able to stand on its own.

And she'd learned her lesson: Tara would never leave herself at the mercy of others, no matter who they were. She would grow strong enough to stand for herself.

Tara would never be a victim again.

# CHAPTER 4

## PRESENT DAY

"I'm sorry," the doctor said to Rex Dexin. He was sitting on the hospital bed with his right elbow in a sling.

Rex shut his eyes for a moment as he absorbed the news. It was over. The years he'd spent riding the saddle and ranch bronc rodeo circuits had come to an end. The damage to his elbow this time was too great—a severe ligament tear on both ends of his ulnar as well as a significant damage to the nerve there that had now affected his grip strength. And even though surgery could get it all fixed, the doctor had made it clear that bronc riding was not in his future if he still wanted to retain normal use of his elbow for everyday ranch needs.

He let out an exhale. Rex had joined the circuit

many years ago as a way to deal with his sorrows. And it had worked. Once he was on that horse, fighting to keep his seat and risking his life, nothing else mattered. And since he was bone-tired by the end of the event, it got him some reprieve from the sleepless nights that often haunted him. But more than that, Rex had come to love the event—it was just him and the horse moving as one.

Rex had known he'd have to quit the circuit one day, but he hadn't expected that to be now. But yet again, he'd lost something he loved—and he had no say in the matter.

He ran his left hand through his hair and sighed. He would have to learn to deal with it like always, though it wouldn't be easy.

He opened his eyes and looked at the doctor, a middle-aged man with salt-and-pepper hair. "So when will the surgery be?" Rex asked.

"Tomorrow," the doctor replied. "The sooner we fix this, the better. Why don't I give you some time to think about what we've discussed? I'll come back later and we can sign the consent forms then."

"Sounds good," Rex said. "Thanks."

"My pleasure," the doctor responded. Then he patted Rex's shoulder and headed toward the room's exit.

Rex watched him leave and shut the door behind him.

But before he could relax, the door swung open again, and his three business partners rushed in.

Rex had been fortunate to meet Weston and Liam Grayson at one of the Texas rodeo events Rex had ridden in a couple of years ago. They'd hit it off, and only a dinner later, Rex had signed a partnership agreement with the two brothers to start a horse breeding operation.

And his instincts had paid off. The business had done better than they'd expected, and Cole, the brothers' younger cousin, had joined them a few months later. DexGray Horse Ranch had grown over the years and was now the premier source of horses of the highest quality in the region. Thankfully, Rex's injury wasn't going to affect the running of the business in any way.

"So what did the doc say?" Weston, the oldest of the trio, asked as he crammed his solid frame into one of the visitors' chairs. Rex was surprised the chair didn't collapse.

Rex leaned back on the pillow. "No more bronc riding for me. And I need surgery to fix this." He pointed to his injured elbow. They'd become as close as brothers, so telling them wasn't a big deal. But saying the words out loud still slammed a world of hurt into Rex's heart.

"Are you okay?" Liam asked from where he'd leaned against a wall. He was the quiet one in the group but had a way of getting right to the heart of a matter.

Rex gave him a tentative smile. "Not yet, but I will be."

"It's about time you quit riding," Cole stated from where he'd taken a spot on the bed. It was just like him to say what was on his mind. "What?" His eyes narrowed at Weston as he rubbed his shin. Weston must have kicked him there. Then he turned back to Rex. "I know you enjoyed the sport, but we all know you were doing it for all the wrong reasons."

"What do you mean?" Rex asked, his defenses going up. He'd never shared his real motive for bronc riding with any of them—his memories were his burden to carry.

"It's okay, Rex," Liam said. "What Cole is trying to say is that this might be a good time to face your demons, instead of running away from them like you've been doing."

Rex's chest tightened. "I haven't been running—"

"We know about the sleepless nights," Weston

interjected, then in a softer voice, "and about Tammy."

Rex's heart sank. How? He'd never mentioned Tammy. Ever. That was tantamount to shattering the already fragile wall that kept the memories in. But then he felt a momentary sense of relief. They at least didn't know about Rose.

"You spoke about her the night you had the fever a few months ago," Liam said.

Rex remembered that day. A hurricane had come through and blown the roof off one of their horse barns, and Rex had gotten soaked in the downpour as he'd helped move the spooked horses from that barn to a dry one. The effort had taken hours, and Rex had ended up with a fever. He'd woken up the next morning to see the guys in his room and had surmised they'd helped get his fever down, but he'd had no idea he'd muttered stuff while in the throes of it. The guys had never mentioned it either.

He closed his eyes. They knew about Tammy. The second person he'd failed.

Rex felt his heart squeeze in hurt at the thought of her. He'd been barely holding it together since Rose's death. But then it had gotten easier to live and breathe each day—having his family around him had helped, and soon he'd found joy again.

Then Tammy had needed him. Rex had chosen her—he couldn't fail anyone again after Rose. Yet he'd ended up hurting his family instead, something he'd regretted ever since.

And Tammy had died.

It had been a massive blow to him, and Rex wasn't sure he'd ever get over it. With his family no longer by his side, he'd needed a way to let it all out. So he'd started ranch bronc riding, and then saddle bronc riding when the former wasn't enough.

"I think it's time to deal with everything," Weston said quietly. "Tammy. Your family. I know it's going to be hard, but you won't be alone."

*No.* He couldn't tackle any of it now. Rex would take care of his elbow, and that was it. Nothing more. Everything else needed to stay buried. There was no point in stirring the hornet's nest. But what did Weston mean he wouldn't be alone?

"And to that end, I think it's time we consider moving back to the east coast," Weston said.

Rex's eyes flipped open, and he straightened, grimacing at the pain in his elbow. "What?" They'd talked about it on and off, but it had seemed like a plan for the future. Definitely not now. "Why?"

"It's not for your sake alone," Cole said. "Grandma called us while you were still riding in the event and threatened to send Hayford after us if we didn't come home soon." He shuddered.

Rex fought to hide his smile. The guys had told him horror stories about their grandma's butler in Boston and how *efficient* he was at getting things done. As far as the butler was concerned, their grandma's word was law, and he followed it to the letter no matter what it took—even if it meant dragging in the guys kicking and screaming. His partners wouldn't survive the attack. "But why now?"

"She said we need to give her grandbabies before she kicks the bucket," Liam said. Rex's eyebrow rose. "Her words not mine. Also a close family friend's son is getting married in Dexington in two months, and she's commanded us to be there. We can't ignore her request this time."

Dexington wasn't that far from Dexin where Rex grew up. Was this God letting him know it was time for him to make amends with his family and face the music of what he'd done? But wait! He didn't have to go. The guys could return to the east coast without him. He could stay in Texas and manage the business on their behalf.

Liam crushed that idea almost as soon as Rex thought of it. "Rex, the electronic wedding invite Grandma forwarded also has your name on it. She made sure you were included, which means you can't dodge it," he said as if guessing Rex's thoughts. "The physical invite is on its way to us in the mail."

"Regardless of the wedding, I believe we should use this opportunity to open an East Coast operation like we've always talked about," Weston said to Rex. "And I think we should look into Dexin Valley. It has the kind of land we'll need, and it's your home territory as well. You'll also get a chance to reconnect with your family. We know you've missed them."

"And we'll be close to Grandma without being directly under her nose," Cole said. "The alternative would be disastrous." He shuddered again.

"So we pacify Grandma, you make up with your family, *and* we start a new chapter of our business," Liam said. "It would be a win-win-win for all of us." He folded his arms across his chest. "So what do you think?"

It was obvious they'd come prepared for this conversation, and it seemed this was one time he wouldn't win. Besides, they should have opened the East Coast operation a few years ago and had only held back because of him. Yet they couldn't go ahead without his say-so—it was how they made all their decisions. But he could see this was something they wanted, and it was for his benefit too.

"But what about our business here?" Rex asked. "Two months isn't enough to take care of everything here adequately." And it was too little time to prepare to see his family.

"What do you think about having Patrick run the business here?" Weston asked. Patrick was the current manager in charge of the day-to-day operations and had done a wonderful job ever since he was hired. His previous years of experience in running a ranch had been a bonus.

"We don't have to hand over operations to him completely within two months, though I believe he's more than able to handle it on his own within that time frame," Weston continued. "But we can always come back and check in on him every now and then. We'll also need to secure a place on the East Coast for our new business and transition some of our operations there, and I expect that would take time too."

Rex agreed their business would be in good hands if Patrick was placed in charge of it. But they'd built this partnership painstakingly from the ground up, and this was a decision Rex couldn't make lightly. Besides, he wasn't sure he was ready to face his family. Or for the unknown reception he'd receive.

"Let me think about it," he said.

"That's a fine idea, though I believe you'll agree

with us in the end," Cole said. "I think this is God telling you to take a break."

"I agree with Pastor Cole," Weston said with a chuckle.

"Once again, you guys won't take me seriously," Cole muttered under his breath. Liam and Weston laughed.

Rex leaned back. He had a lot to think about and decisions to make.

But right now, he needed to get through the surgery first.

Rex alighted from a private plane two months later, all dressed in a three-piece suit with his wheeled carry-on bag and its cylindrical attachment in one hand and a drawstring bag with his cowboy hat in it in the other. He soon reached the bottom of the steps, dropped the carry-on, and pulled out his phone. Now where was the car he'd hired?

Weston, Liam, and Cole had left the week before to visit their family in Boston before heading down to Dexington for the wedding. Rex could have gone with them, since Dexin—his hometown—was close enough to both Dexington and Boston, but he'd chosen to stay back in an attempt to delay his trip home as much as possible. Though he'd never been afraid to take risks, the thought of meeting up with his family scared him. So he'd ended up arriving in Dexington on the day of the wedding. He'd figured it was better to get the marriage ceremony he'd been invited to out of the way first before coming up with a plan on how to approach his family.

Especially since Rex had been the cause of the rift between them.

Rex had left town with Tammy, his brother's girl-friend at the time, and was sure the betrayal had hurt his older brother, Max. But none of his family knew the real truth: Rex had done it for Max's own sake.

And now he was back to face the music.

He tugged at the tie at his neck even as he fished out his phone from his pocket. Rex hated dressing up like this, but Grandma Grayson had insisted on the attire when she'd video-chatted with him and the guys a month ago. She'd guessed they would try to wear their cowboy hats with jeans otherwise. Rex had managed to convince himself he could suffer through a few hours of it.

But he'd forgotten how hot it could be in the summer, and the tie was practically choking him.

Rex glanced around. Now where was his car

again? He'd hired one instead of renting since he'd be with the guys later, and they already had enough cars between them. Even though his elbow had healed well, Rex tried to avoid driving whenever he could for the time being.

He powered on his phone and noticed a voicemail waiting for him. Rex listened to it and grimaced. The town car he'd hired—a one-man operation that had come highly recommended—couldn't make it. The driver's wife had gone into labor, and all the other town car services were fully booked because of an event in town. Fortunately, the driver had managed to secure an SUV for him from one of the rental companies.

Rex tucked his phone into his pocket. The news wasn't what he'd expected, but he'd roll with it. As it was, he was already late for the wedding.

So he grabbed his carry-on and headed into the airport terminal to pick up his car.

## CHAPTER 5

Tara Ellis reviewed the MRI preliminary report on the screen in front of her one more time, clicked the approve button, and then signed out of the electronic medical records.

She leaned back in her swivel chair and let out an exhale. Thank goodness her shift at the New York hospital as the on-site attending radiologist for the overnight float was finally over. Though it'd been a busy one, Tara and her senior resident had handled the cases so efficiently they'd been on-track to finish the call on time.

But an emergency case had arrived in the ER during her checkout session at the tail-end of the shift, and rather than hand it off to the next attending

—who was due to arrive in a few minutes—Tara had supervised her senior resident as he conducted the MRI procedure on the twenty-year-old patient, who it turned out had developed acute necrotizing pancreatitis that was already septic. She'd called the referring clinician with the urgent findings while praying the patient would survive and be alright.

But the extra procedure had meant she'd stayed longer at the hospital than planned.

There was a knock on the door, and Tara looked up.

Krissy, a radiology fellow and one of her good friends at the hospital, stood by the entrance of the attending reading area, the room which Tara had been working in. "I thought you'll be gone by now," she said as she tucked her short blonde curls behind her ears and made her way to Tara.

Tara stretched her tired arms above her head. "I thought I'll be too, but you know how it is."

"Bad case?"

Tara nodded. "I'm sure the surgeons can handle it."

"I pray it goes well too." Krissy perched at the edge of Tara's workstation. "So the vacation begins, huh?"

Tara grinned. "One month of glorious peace."

"And wedding planning."

"Yes, that too." Tara's best friend, Zoey, was engaged and needed Tara's help to plan her wedding. Tara was supposed to meet up with her today in Dexington at a marriage ceremony Zoey was part of, and then return with her to Dexin—a town that was a few hours away from Dexington—where Tara would spend the rest of her vacation.

"Maybe you'll meet a cowboy of your own like Zoey did," Krissy said. Zoey had met her fiancé, Dex, during her first vacation to Dexin before she'd decided to settle there.

"Nope, not interested," Tara said. Relationships and marriage were off-limits for her. She planned to remain single for the rest of her life.

"That's what Zoey said too," Krissy said. Krissy had met Zoey on one of her lunch dates with Tara, and they'd all become good friends.

Tara smacked Krissy's leg. "Get off my table if you're going to utter nonsense."

Krissy jumped off and laughed. "I'll be sure to remind you of this moment when you go all moon-eyed at the cowboy. I can imagine him now—tall, dark, and broody. The bad boy type."

Tara chuckled in disbelief. "You're crazy." Then she checked her time and rushed to her feet. "Oh my goodness! I'm going to be late!" She had to hurry if she had any hope of getting a shower in before racing to the airport. She reached for the research papers stacked on the work surface in front of her and stuffed them into her satchel.

"Okay, okay, I'll get out of your hair," Krissy said. She strode to the door but turned as she reached it. "Go hook that cowboy, *sistar*," she said with a wink. Then she flounced out of the room.

Tara shook her head, a sad smile playing on her lips. This was one wish that was never going to come true.

Tara sprinted down the airport escalator as fast as she could. She was already running late. She'd ended up missing her flight from New York to Dexington, and she hadn't been able to reach Zoey either. Yet it was better to be there late than never, so she'd hopped on the next available flight, and here she was.

Zoey and her fiancé, Dex, were part of the wedding train, and since Dex's whole family was attending the event, Zoey had thought it would be a great opportunity for Tara to meet them all. She'd gone on and on about how great they were, which got Tara curious. Her own experiences of family had always been those of disappointment and failure, so she was keen to witness for herself what made them special.

Her best friend had also gushed about how much fun she'd had helping out with the wedding planning for what was slated to be the biggest celebrity wedding in Dexington. Three of the city's most eligible bachelors were getting married on the same day, and Zoey had wanted to share the experience with Tara. Since Zoey was the sister of her heart, Tara had obliged.

She figured she could make the tail end of the wedding if she hurried, especially since she didn't need to change outfits to get ready for the wedding—Tara wore a high-necked navy-blue lace midi dress with long sleeves and a detachable belt, paired with a gold clutch and high heels.

Tara soon reached the end of the escalator and made her way across the main floor of the arrival terminal with her carry-on bag in her left hand. Though she was primarily here for the wedding and to spend her overdue vacation with Zoey, she also wanted to meet Dex and make sure he was worthy of Zoey.

But marriage was a step Tara had no plans to take herself. She didn't deserve a family of her own, didn't want to depend on anyone else, and couldn't afford to have her heart broken again.

But this was not the time to be thinking about all this.

She had a wedding to make, so Tara hurried toward the rental car counter even as she tried to reach Zoey again.

"I'm sorry, ma'am, but there are no cars left," the agent at the rental car sales counter said to Tara.

"But I had a car booked!" Tara protested.

"Yes, you did, ma'am, but unfortunately you didn't arrive at the time you'd specified, and with a big event in town today, all the cars in your requested category have been taken."

"Are there any other cars available? I don't mind paying for an upgrade."

"Let me check." The young lady with the short bob standing behind the counter scanned the screen in front of her. Then she looked up at Tara. "We do have an SUV available, but it's the last one."

Tara's shoulders relaxed. "I'll take it." SUVs weren't her first preference, but beggars couldn't be choosers.

She just needed a vehicle that would get her to the wedding as fast as possible.

# CHAPTER 6

Rex approached a free agent at the rental counter. "Good morning," he said. "I'm here to pick up my car."

The agent, a young lady in a black T-shirt and pants gave him an appreciative glance. "Good morning, sir," she replied. "What's the name on the reservation?"

"Rex Dexin."

"Thank you." She typed in some information on the computer in front of her and then frowned. "One minute please." She turned to her colleague on the right and whispered some words to her.

Rex observed the exchange. Was something wrong with the booking too? He hoped not, since he had to meet up with the guys soon, before the wedding ended.

Then the agent returned to him. "I'll get you all set up shortly," she said.

"Is anything the matter?" he asked.

She gave him a warm smile. "Just a mix-up, but it's been taken care of. Can I have your driver's license please?"

Rex's shoulders relaxed. *Good*. He still had a car. He pulled his wallet from his pocket and handed over the license to her. Then she slid some paperwork to him, which he began to fill out.

"What?" Rex heard a loud voice say on his right. He looked up from what he'd been working on only to see a stunning woman in a blue dress that flattered her figure drumming her fingers on the counter. Based on her side profile, she looked like she could very well have walked off the pages of a magazine. "You must be joking."

Then she turned her face in his direction, and Rex's heart skipped a beat. Gosh, she was beautiful with those gorgeous brown eyes, even though she had fury written all over her face—and even if it appeared to be directed at him. Yet she looked vaguely familiar. Had he met her before? But then she focused back on her customer service rep.

"What's going on?" Rex asked his agent.

"Uhm… like I said there was some mix-up," she replied. "Your car appeared to be available, so my colleague had mistakenly offered it to her."

Rex grimaced. That must suck for her. Unfortunately he couldn't give up the car—the guys and even their grandma would never let him hear the end of it if he was a no-show. Rex hoped the rental service had an alternate solution for her.

"I can't believe you have no car for me," he heard the beautiful customer say. "So when is the next car going to be available?"

"I'm sorry, ma'am, but we don't have any cars returning until later in the evening."

*Yikes*. That must be frustrating.

"This is insane," the customer said, running her hands through her hair. Glorious hair, he might add.

But this was not the time to be distracted. As Rex completed his paperwork and handed it over, he could hear the other counter rep apologizing to the lady over and over again.

The agent in front of him accepted the papers from Rex, reached behind her on the cork board to retrieve the car keys, and then offered them to him.

Rex reached for the keys, but then a hand

clamped over his. "I believe this is mine." It was the beautiful customer.

Was she crazy? Sure, the rental company had done her wrong, but it had nothing to do with him. "I'm sorry?"

"You heard me," she said. "I was here first, and I believe this is my car."

"Ma'am, *this is my* car. Reserved under my name. Please let go." Rex disliked it when people were rude, female or not.

"I can't do that," she said, her chocolate eyes spitting out fire.

"Ma'am, please restrain yourself and remove your hand." Rex could have given up the keys and then tried to find an available cab that would take him to his destination, but he hated bullies of any kind. He'd assumed the lady was a person of character; apparently he was wrong. Rex could easily pry her hand off, but he preferred to give her a chance to retain her dignity.

"Restrain myself? Are you kidding me?"

By now, they were drawing glances from other folks passing by in the terminal. This wasn't the way Rex had planned for his morning to go, and time was ticking.

Then an idea occurred to him.

"What if I dropped you off at your destination?" he asked. "Is that okay with you?"

# CHAPTER 7

Tara stared at the obnoxious handsome man who'd made her the offer. She was mad at him for stealing the car they'd been about to give her, and now he was offering her a ride? Despite her anger at the man, she had to admit he looked hot in that three-piece suit that molded perfectly on his fit body. He even had that bad boy look she secretly liked. But from what she knew, most guys that looked like bad boys were actually bad boys. And she'd never met him before. What if he was a serial killer? What if he wanted to exact revenge on her for embarrassing him? Tara would be playing right into his hands.

She was all ready to refuse him, but then she remembered how disappointed Zoey would feel if Tara didn't show up at all for the wedding. It was all she'd had been talking about for weeks. Tara could endure a ride with the stranger for Zoey. Besides, she wasn't helpless anymore—she had a black belt in Brazilian Jiu-Jitsu and also had her trusty pepper spray in her clutch. She already disliked the man, but she could endure him for the next thirty minutes or however long the trip was.

"Ma'am, is that okay with you?" he asked again.

"Sure. That's fine," Tara finally said. Then she removed her hand.

"Great!" the counter agent who had been attending to her said with relief written all over her face. "Thank you, sir, for the offer. We're more than happy to make this car free for you for the inconvenience."

"It's fine, you don't have to do that," the man said. "You can put the bill on my tab."

"Thank you, sir. Have a great trip. You too, ma'am."

The man turned to Tara. "Can I help you with your bag, Miss…?"

"Just call me Tara," she said. "Thanks for the offer, but I can carry my bag just fine."

"Okay. And I'm Rex. Nice to meet you." He offered her his hand.

Nice name, and it seemed he wanted to make peace. Tara hadn't forgiven him, but she could accept a truce if it meant she would get a ride. So she accepted the handshake, which was firm just like she'd expected.

Except for the jolt of electricity that coursed through her arm at his touch.

She dropped his hand and turned so Rex couldn't see her burning face. What was that all about? He was a stranger for goodness' sake. "Let's get going," she managed to say.

Tara didn't wait for his response and followed the signs that led to where the elevators would be. She heard footsteps behind her and assumed it was Rex even as she halted in front of the elevators that led to the underground parking lot. And before she could, a large hand reached past her and pressed the elevator button.

The elevator arrived almost immediately, and Tara stepped in. Rex did the same. The guy seemed to fill the elevator with his presence, but she ignored him and stared straight ahead. But as the elevator doors were about to close, a hand reached out and stopped it.

"Excuse me," a pot-bellied man wearing a white

shirt with billowy sleeves over brown breeches said as he led a large group into the elevator.

Tara moved to the back of the elevator, pulling her carry-on luggage to her side, and watched as members of the party piled in. They all wore one form of Renaissance outfit or another, as if they were off to some Renaissance festival. Maybe that was the event that had caused the rental company to run out of vehicles.

But then a very masculine and unapologetic scent, with a hint of woody musk and leather enveloped her. Tara turned to see Rex standing right next to her other side, closer than she'd have expected.

The butterflies in her stomach began to flutter. What was it about this man that he affected her so? Tara had shied away from relationships over the years, and it had suited her just fine. Of course she'd had admirers, but none that made her want to inhale their scent—like she did with this man.

Tara turned away from him. *No!* She couldn't allow herself to think such weird thoughts.

Then the elevator lurched, and suddenly a tidal wave of bodies slammed into her, knocking her off her feet.

Tara's arms flailed as she fought to regain her

stance. Instead, she flew forward and soon smacked into a solid body in front of her, her face landing on another's.

Tara froze. No, it couldn't be.

She heard a collective gasp that affirmed that what she'd thought a dream had really happened.

Tara blinked as she stared into the pools of chocolate that was Rex's eyes.

Her lips smashed against his.

Which, by the way, were surprisingly soft.

Tara's face and neck grew warm. She gasped just as he pulled back, jerking against the wall of bodies that had slammed into her from behind in the tightly packed elevator, the scent of strong perfumes warring with the disinfectant smell that was native to the elevator.

She took a deep breath as she fought to hide her mortification. "I'm sorry," she managed to mutter, turning her face down to hide it from view. *This is so embarrassing!* Tara wished she could just shrink into a ball and roll away. What would he think of her now?

*Calm down, Tara*, she thought to herself. *No need to panic.*

"Are you alright?" Rex asked, his deep voice stealing past her defenses and reaching right into her.

Why did he sound so nice when all she wanted to do was disappear from here—where she was the center of unwanted attention—and pop up in the women's bathroom?

Instead, Tara nodded as she fought the urge to look up and stare into the eyes she felt searching her face. She ran her hands through her hair and then reached for her carry-on bag, which thankfully seemed to have made it through the bump just fine.

Unlike her.

Her face was probably red all over.

How was she going to look him in the eye now?

The elevators arrived at the parking level, and the large party piled out. A few gave her quick smiles, and Tara wished she could just disappear. She was pretty sure the accidental kiss was going to be fodder for entertainment on their way to the festival. But she would never see them again, as opposed to the man she'd kissed, who she still had to ride with. Tara still couldn't believe she'd kissed Rex. But more importantly, Tara didn't like how she'd enjoyed the kiss a little.

*Ugh! Tara, you can't be thinking about this*, she chastised herself. Maybe it was better to stay as far away from him as possible and pretend the kiss never happened.

Rex held the elevator door open for her, and Tara stepped out. She noted with relief that he said nothing about the kiss. He led the way until they reached the red SUV parked in the leftmost corner of the lot, and then he pressed the key fob.

The trunk popped open, and Tara headed back there to put in her overnight bag. But Rex grabbed it before she could.

"I can do it myself," she said.

"I insist," he replied before placing it in the trunk and then dropping his own in as well, hedging in a smaller cylindrical bag as if wanting to keep it secure. Then he shut the trunk.

Tara returned to the passenger side to get in, but then she noticed Rex had already opened the door for her. Why was he being so nice all of a sudden? Tara hadn't expected such good manners from him. Or was it because of the kiss? She hoped not.

"Thanks," she said. "But I can open my own doors."

Rex said nothing and waited for her to enter before shutting the door after her. She had a feeling he'd ignore her words and do it again if the occasion arose.

Tara watched him drop the drawstring bag in the back seat before taking the driver's seat. They both secured their seat belts, while Rex also adjusted his seat and steering wheel positions to accommodate his long legs. Finally, he turned the ignition.

Then he turned to her, his brown eyes settling on her face. Tara fought the urge to look away.

"Where should I take you?" he asked.

"To Dexington House," Tara replied.

Rex froze.

# CHAPTER 8

Rex stilled at her words. He couldn't believe they were going to the same place. First the kiss and now the same destination? How was that even possible?

He hadn't dated in a while, so the kiss, however accidental, had been a shock. It was like everything else had faded except for the two of them in that moment, and he'd felt a longing for more. Her scent—the smell of summer, of coconuts and beaches and sea salt, with hints of vanilla—had warmed him in its embrace, and all he'd wanted to do was remain there with her.

But he'd forced himself to pull away from her and step back—she was a stranger after all. Yet why had this kiss affected him so? Maybe he only felt this way because he hadn't kissed anyone for a long time. Besides, he couldn't forget how annoying she'd been at the car rental counter. Character was everything, no matter how beautiful she was, and she'd shown him she was lacking in it.

He'd considered apologizing for the kiss, but it hadn't been intentional, and Rex felt it might call more attention to it—something it seemed she didn't want, since she'd also kept mute about the kiss. It seemed as if it'd meant nothing to her, or maybe she preferred to pretend it'd never happened. Which was fine by him, since he wanted nothing more to do with her. He'd thought he'd drop her off, and that would be it.

And now they were headed to the same place.

Well, the wedding was supposed to be large enough that they'd probably not run into each other again. Good thing he'd only planned to stay a few hours before heading to his hotel.

"Is anything the matter?" she asked.

"No," Rex replied. There was no benefit to letting her know they were going to the same destination.

"Okay. So here's the address," she said, handing him the gold-embossed invitation card. Though Rex had already memorized the address before the trip, he glanced at the card before returning it to her and then inputting the address into the car's GPS. Then he drove out of the airport.

Tara remained quiet throughout the ride into town, and that suited Rex just fine. He stared out the window as they passed through the quaint and picturesque areas of Dexington, which was known for its large historic country homes, brick-lined streets, and colonial structures. Yet Rex believed Dexin with its rolling hills and meadows was far prettier.

Soon they arrived at Dexington Street, and Rex could see the sprawling mansion with its massive gates up ahead. A few security checkpoints had been set up before they could approach the estate. Tara passed her invitation card and her driver's license to him, and Rex presented them at the first checkpoint along with his own. The guard scanned the QR code at the back of the invitation, waited for the green beep of the device he held, and scanned their driver's licenses before waving them through.

It seemed the card contained a hidden code that was only present in authentic versions. That was genius, by the way, but Rex was certain he'd never need that in his life. Marriage was nowhere on his list right now, and even then, Rex would prefer a quiet intimate event with friends and family.

They went through two similar checks, and then they arrived at the mansion.

# CHAPTER 9

*T*ara fought to keep her mouth closed as the large estate gates swung open at their approach. Zoey had said the Dexingtons were rich, but Tara hadn't imagined they were *that* rich.

The wrought-iron gates were the most beautiful she'd ever seen with their intricate leaf design, so detailed it must have taken months to create them. And that was only the beginning. Then there were the stunning manicured gardens—ethereal like something out of a fairytale storybook—surrounding a fountain running from an angel's water jar into a pool beneath it, and the curved cobblestone driveway, all leading up to the largest mansion she'd ever seen.

A valet took another look at her invitation card and then gave them permission to drive up the sectioned-off circular driveway, which was a different area from where other guests were being steered to. Soon they reached the top, and Rex parked the car at the far end of the lot.

Tara got out, adjusting and smoothing her dress. A quick run of her hand through her hair and a peek at the side mirror confirmed she still looked presentable. Rex exited from the car as well, pulled her bag from the trunk, and brought it to her side.

"Thank you," Tara said, accepting the bag. "And thanks for the ride."

"You're welcome."

There was an awkward moment, but then Tara said, "I'm sure you can find your way out."

"I'll take care of it," Rex said.

"Okay, bye." She didn't wait for his response and left, making her way to the mansion's entrance. Tara had finally gotten Zoey on the phone on her way to the rental counter, and she'd told her to come straight to the main house. Soon she reached the front entrance and pressed the doorbell.

But then she heard light footsteps and whirled around.

Her eyes widened. Rex was right behind her.

"What are you doing?" she asked harshly. "Are you stalking me?" This was what she had to deal with when it came to strangers. You never knew when they would turn against you.

Tara dropped her carry-on bag and moved into a defensive stance. "You're not allowed here," she said. "Please get off this property or I'm going to call security. In fact, I'm going to do that right now." She pulled out her phone.

Zoey had insisted Tara program the security team's number into the phone in case she got held up at the security checkpoints. Thank goodness she had it now, even though she could have handled this moron just fine, broad shoulders or not. Taking him down would be a no-brainer with her skills, even though he looked very fit and was much bigger than her. Size didn't matter in this case—she had the strength to put him on the ground.

Then one of the doors swung open behind her, and Tara heard a loud gasp.

# CHAPTER 10

Rex froze. He couldn't believe who was standing in front of him. Sure, he looked older, taller, and more mature, but he could recognize his twin brother, Jax, anywhere. And in that moment, it hit him how much he'd missed. Rex and Jax had only been in their early twenties when Rex had left town, and now it was more than a decade later.

"Jax?" he managed to say. Rex was sure he'd driven to Dexington and not to Dexin, and this place didn't look anything like their ranch. So what was Jax doing here? Was this a mirage?

Jax stepped back into the house, his face ashen as if he'd seen a ghost.

No, it probably wasn't a hallucination if Jax was reacting like this. Rex wasn't sure if his twin was going to shut him out and disappear from his view, and since Tara appeared bewildered and had put down her dukes, he quickly side-stepped her and followed Jax into the house.

"Who is it?" a deeper but similarly timbered voice like Rex's asked from beyond Jax. Rex couldn't see who it was. Was it one of his other brothers?

But Jax only shook his head and took another step backward.

Rex's mouth went dry. He didn't know what to say. He'd caused this, created this chasm between him and Jax that now seemed impossible to bridge. They'd been as close as brothers could be, yet Rex had left him suddenly without any explanation. He'd hurt his twin, but he hadn't known to what depths until today. Why had he been so foolish? He should have come back after Tammy died to make amends. Instead, he'd been afraid and stayed away. But Rex hoped it wasn't too late to make things right.

Then the source of the voice that had spoken came into view.

Rex's heart thudded.

*Dex.* His elder brother, who now appeared larger than life, towered over Rex, though Rex was tall enough in his own right.

Dex gasped. "Rex?" His eyes went round like saucers.

Rex's heart barreled against his chest. This was all so sudden. He hadn't expected to see *two* of his brothers here. What was he supposed to say or do?

But Dex saved him by pulling him into a hug. "I can't believe you're here," he said and clapped Rex's shoulder. "It's good to have you back."

"What's going on?" a warm, familiar voice said.

Rex went rigid. He'd recognize that voice anywhere—Rex had followed him around long enough to have it ingrained in his system.

Max, his oldest brother. His hero. The one Rex had always looked up to, and who had stepped in as a father figure to him and his brothers after their pa died, even though he was only a few years older than them.

The room went silent, pregnant with anticipation of what was about to happen.

Dex released Rex and stepped back.

Rex's heart raced as he beheld his oldest brother for the first time in a long time. He looked as handsome as ever, except for some gray at his temples.

He swallowed. This was it, the moment he'd been dreading. Max was the one Rex had hurt the most. What he decided to do would change everything. And

Rex would be okay with it. Because no matter what Max did, Rex deserved it.

But Max pulled him into a hug and held him like he never wanted to let go, like a man holding onto a raft at sea for dear life. Rex was familiar with the story of the prodigal son, but it had never felt more real to him than in this moment.

"I've missed you, little brother," Max said in a choked voice.

Rex's eyes burned with the tears that threatened to flow at the sound of the hurt in Max's voice. It was all his fault. He'd done this and scarred a piece of his beloved brother's soul. "I'm sorry," he managed to say, though the words were not enough to express the depth of his remorse. Then Rex felt a heavy weight—one that had almost crushed him over the years—finally fall away.

He lost track of time as he stood there in Max's arms.

Then Max pulled back and searched his face. "Did you come alone?" he asked. The real question being: where was Tammy?

The memory of Tammy's last moments rushed forward in Rex's mind, and the tears fell. "Yes."

Max pulled him back into a tighter hug. It was like he could see Rex's heart and the truth of what he couldn't bring himself to say. "It's okay. You're back now. That's all that matters."

They stayed that way for a while, the sinner and the saint, Max's forgiveness washing away all the hurt that had existed between them. Sure, there were words that still needed to be said and heard, and this was only the beginning of the healing of their relationship. But it was already much more than Rex had hoped for.

Max finally released Rex and grabbed his hand as if afraid he might disappear at any moment. "There's someone I'd like you to meet," he said, and gestured to a beautiful woman who was standing nearby. She could have passed for a celebrity with her facial features and those stunning green eyes. "Rex, meet my wife, Becca. Becca, meet Rex."

Becca came forward. "Nice to finally meet you," she said with a warm smile. "I've heard so much about you."

"Great to meet you too," Rex said as he returned her smile.

"Daddy!" a loud voice screeched, and Rex turned to see a little girl, all dressed up in a princess dress, barreling toward them and jumping into Max's arms.

Max chuckled. "And this is my adorable Chloe. Chloe, meet Uncle Rex."

"Nice to meet you," Chloe said cheerfully.

Rex couldn't help the grin that split his face. So he had a niece. "Nice to meet you too, Chloe."

Chloe's sparkling blue eyes that looked distinctively like Max's scanned him from head to toe. "Hmm…"

"What is it, Chloe?" Becca asked in amusement.

"Uncle Rex needs pink socks."

The group let out a loud chuckle.

Dex must have noticed Rex's confusion, because he said, "She has a thing for pink socks. We all have to wear them one time or the other. Welcome to the club."

Pink socks? Rex couldn't imagine wearing them, but it was a small price to pay for having such a cute niece.

"Now, I don't think you've met my fiancée, Zoey Brown," Dex said as he ushered forward a stunning young lady Rex hadn't noticed.

Rex raised an eyebrow at Dex. He was getting married? Good for him! "Nice to meet you, Zoey," Rex said.

But Zoey wrapped her arms around him. "Thank goodness you're back," she said. "They've missed you like crazy. All of them." Then she released him.

Rex felt warmth spread through his chest at her words. "Thanks for telling me that."

"You're welcome. Oh, there's one more person I don't think everyone has had a chance to meet." She grabbed Tara's hand and pulled her forward. "Max, Becca, Dex, Jax, this is my best friend Tara."

"Hello, Tara," everyone chorused.

"Nice to meet you all," Tara said with a shy but cheery smile. "I've heard so much about you."

Rex's eyebrows shot up. Was this the same bossy, rude lady from the car rental counter? The same delusional woman that thought Rex was a stalker and had threatened to call security? It was like she had a split personality or something.

But then Zoey's face suddenly turned serious as if a thought had occurred to her, and she turned to Rex. "Did you guys come together?"

# CHAPTER 11

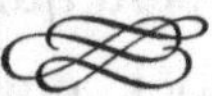

The question flustered Tara. First, she still had a hard time believing that Mr. Obnoxious was related to Zoey's fiancé. Tara had video chatted with Zoey and Dex a few times and had found Dex to be an absolute darling and a gentleman. How could they be brothers?

And now, trust Zoey to have noticed they'd arrived at the same time. Nothing could get past that girlfriend of hers.

"No," she said. "Well, yes. I mean—"

"I gave her a ride from the airport," Rex said. "It just happened that way."

"But I didn't know he was coming to the wedding —or that he had any relation to you all," Tara clarified. "There was only one rental car left at the airport, and we decided to share."

"Yeah, right," Rex muttered under his breath. Tara shot him a dark look.

"Interesting," Zoey said quietly.

Tara gave her a mock glare. "It's not what you think," she hissed, even as she continued to smile at the rest of the group. "I'll explain later."

"I'll be waiting," Zoey whispered back.

"Rex, thank you for doing that," Becca said.

"My pleasure," Rex said.

*Yeah, right.* The car was supposed to have been hers in the first place.

"Why don't we all sit down?" Max said.

"That would be great," Becca said. "My feet are beginning to hurt."

Tara looked around the living room even as Max led them from the cavernous foyer, in which they'd been standing, into the largest living room she'd ever seen. There had to be maids who did the cleaning, since the place was in pristine condition even with its ornate fireplace and central grand winding staircase, mosaic-tile floors, large windows that invited the beauty of the gardens in as part of the decor, and multiple French doors that led to other parts of the home. The result was a stunning, airy space that was an interior designer's dream. *Wow!*

Max directed Becca to the oversized cream sofa in the center of the room.

"That's better," Becca said as she lowered herself onto the couch. Tara liked her at first sight, and she reminded her of the kind of big sister she wished she'd had.

"She's pregnant with our second child," Max said with pride as he sat beside her and tucked Chloe into his other side.

Tara said nothing. Though she was happy for the couple, pregnancy was a topic she never liked to think or talk about.

"Congratulations," Rex said as he claimed one of the love seats. "You must be excited." There was enough seating for everyone, but Zoey pulled Tara to one that was slightly further away yet still within earshot and motioned to Dex to sit with his brothers. Dex obliged with a grin.

"We are," Max said. "And what about you? Are you married?"

"No," Rex replied. The word hung heavy in the air. It felt like there was something not being said.

Tara glanced at Rex. His face appeared calm, but she could see the muscle twitch in his jaw. There was definitely something going on! It seemed Rex had baggage he didn't want to talk about, just like her.

*Oh, don't start, Tara,* she scolded herself. *Have you forgotten how disagreeable he was before? Besides, relationships and marriage are off the table for you.*

But wait! Was the wedding done if everyone was gathered here? They all seemed to be dressed in wedding outfits, though some looked more askew, like Max's and Becca's, than others. "Is the wedding over?" she whispered to Zoey.

"The main ceremony is," Zoey whispered back. "The reception is going on right now, but we'd had enough, so it seemed we all slipped out. Becca has enough people to handle it, so she's not worried about not being there. The house, however, is off-limits to guests except family."

Tara's eyebrows rose. "Family? Is Dex related to the Dexingtons?"

"It's a long story. I'll tell you later. After you tell me what the deal is with you and Rex."

"There's nothing between us," Tara replied. Then she remembered the kiss, and her ears burned.

"Uh-huh," Zoey cocked her head. "Now why do I smell a lie?"

There was no way Tara was admitting to the kiss.

The best defense was an offense. "Why are you trying to pair me off? I like my life just the way it is."

"Okay, I'm going to back off," Zoey said. "But don't think this conversation is over." She gave Tara a quick hug. "I'm glad you made it. I can't wait to spend the next few weeks with you."

Tara's shoulders relaxed. Zoey was like a bulldog when she was after something. "I'm glad I'm here too. But what about the girls? You promised to introduce me to them." Zoey had met the brides when they'd come down to the Dexin Ranch to plan their wedding with Becca, and they'd hit it off. It hadn't hurt that the brides were doctors just like Zoey and Tara.

"They decided to ditch the rest of the reception and head out early for their honeymoon," Zoey said. "Those girls aren't the partying type." Tara didn't blame them—she wasn't either. "But there's going to be a slumber party when they come back. We can have you come down from New York if you want."

A slumber party sounded fun. "But how was the wedding?"

"Fantastic. The vows brought tears to my eyes. It made me wish mine was soon too."

Tara stared at her friend in surprise. Zoey had never been big on marriage after her sister stole her ex-fiancé. Now she couldn't wait to get married? Tara hoped she wouldn't catch the marriage bug.

"Seriously though, Tara, you need to find a nice young man that would treat you right."

"I'm not interested."

"It's because you haven't met the right guy," Zoey said. She glanced at Rex.

"Don't start," Tara said, putting a halt to whatever Zoey had been about to say.

"Okay. But you need to meet more eligible men. And there were a few who caught my eye at the wedding."

Tara stared at her friend in disbelief. Couldn't she just let the topic die? "Zoey? Seriously?"

The French doors behind them opened.

# CHAPTER 12

"We've been looking for you!" a familiar voice said, and Rex turned to see Weston, Liam, and Cole coming through a set of French doors.

Rex rose to his feet and strode forward. He reached Weston first and clapped him on the back. "Yes, I made it."

"Thank goodness," Liam said, relief written all over his face. "Now you can save me from Grandma. She's driving me mad with all her matchmaking."

"Grandma has been introducing him to all the young, single women at the wedding," Cole said.

"She just wants the best for you," Rex said, his lips twitching up in a smile.

"Yeah, right," Liam said. "Now she can be on your case instead."

"Wait, did we interrupt something?" Weston said, looking from Rex to everyone seated in the room. Then his eyes widened. "Is that—?"

"Come on, let me introduce you to my family." Rex led them to where everyone sat. "Everyone, meet my business partners and friends, Weston, Liam, and Cole. Weston and Liam are brothers, and Cole is their cousin. Weston, meet my brothers: Max, Dex, and Jax." Dex and Jax both gave them nods. Max rose to his feet and extended his hand to Weston first. "Nice to meet you."

Weston gave him a firm handshake. "A pleasure."

Then Max shook Liam's and Cole's hands as well. The guys muttered their greetings.

"And this is Becca, Max's wife, and their adorable daughter, Chloe," Rex continued.

"Hello," Becca said with a gentle smile. The guys dipped their heads at her.

"Then we have Zoey, Dex's fiancée."

"Hi." Zoey gave the guys a small wave. They nodded in her direction.

"And that's Tara, sitting next to her." Rex was surprised to see her smile at them, and even more shocked when the guys returned her smile.

A pang of jealousy ran through him. Wait, why was he reacting this way? The lady meant nothing to him, nothing at all. But still, Rex couldn't shake off that feeling. So he turned to Weston. "Where's Grandma?"

"Still mixing and mingling."

"And I hope she stays there," Cole said. Liam smacked the back of his head. "What? As if that's not what you want."

"Sorry about that," Liam said to Rex's family. "He has a habit of saying whatever pops into his mind."

Dex chuckled. "Not a problem. Jax here is like that."

But Jax said nothing. And come to think of it, Jax hadn't said much since Rex arrived, which was not in keeping with his personality, at least as Rex knew it. It seemed Jax still had an axe to grind with him. Rex would have to make time to speak to him privately.

Weston smiled at Rex's brothers. "Wow! Who would have thought Rex would meet you here? Did he tell you we were planning to come over to Dexin soon?"

"We haven't gotten to that part yet," Rex said.

"You should still come to Dexin," Max said.

"And you're welcome to stay at the ranch. A friend of Rex is a friend of ours."

Rex couldn't help feeling good at his words. That was one of the things he'd always loved about Max—he was very accepting of others.

"Do you mind if we sit with you?" Weston asked.

"Not at all," Max said. "Please."

The guys crammed themselves into another smaller couch in the space. But before they could settle in, the French doors opened again.

All eyes swung in that direction, and everyone including Rex jumped to their feet.

It was Grandma Grayson also known as Iron Lady marching in their direction with another grand old lady at her side. She looked exquisite with her usual silver bob and wore a cream coat over a pale pink embroidered gown paired with pink heels. A set of pearls graced her neck.

"Grandma!" Cole said as the ladies reached them.

"Grandma Helen," Dex, Jax, and Becca said in unison with a smile to the lady beside Grandma Grayson.

"There you are!" Grandma Grayson said. "I've been looking all over for you." She turned to the lady by her side. "These are my grandchildren. This one, this one, and that one," she said, pointing to Weston, Liam, and Cole respectively. "And this one, Rex, I've adopted," she said. "Boys, now say hello to Helen. This is her house, and she's the grandmother of one of the grooms."

"Of all of them, actually. I adopted the other two," the lady called Grandma Helen said with a twinkle in her eye. She looked like royalty with her white hair sculptured in place and her perfectly tailored high-collared coat dress with pocket detailing, open at the neck to reveal her jeweled choker.

So this was the woman that held the reins of the Dexington family.

"Good day, ma'am," the guys said as one.

"Oh my, such handsome gentlemen." Grandma Helen turned to Grandma Grayson. "You're right. We need to get them all married off." Then she gestured to Max. "Have you met the other half of my family, the Dexins? Meet Max and his wife, Becca, Dex, and Jax."

His family was related to the Dexingtons? Who would have thought? No wonder they were at the wedding. He'd have to get the full story from his brothers some other time.

"Nice to meet you, ma'am," Max said to Grandma Grayson. His brothers echoed the same.

Then Grandma Helen's eyes swept over Rex. "Oh my, you look just like them. You are…?"

"Rex Dexin, ma'am."

"Ah, the missing Rex. And you're cute too." She reached out and pinched his cheeks.

Rex heard a chuckle coming from his side. It had to be Tara. He forced back a sigh. Oh the things he had to endure for grandmothers. He waited until she released him.

Grandma Helen turned to Grandma Grayson. "Now we need to come up with a plan to get them all married this year. With your three… no four… and Jax, that should be enough to keep us busy for the rest of the year."

This year? That had to be a joke. Rex wasn't ready for marriage, and he wasn't sure he'd ever be.

"I agree," Grandma Grayson said. "These boys need all the help they can get."

Another needling grandmother on top of the one he already had to deal with? Rex exchanged glances with the guys, their faces mirroring the same concern. This was getting dangerous. He needed to divert their attention from their eligibility.

Rex faced Grandma Grayson. "Grandma—"

"And who is this pretty lady?" Grandma Grayson had set her eyes on Tara.

"I'm Tara Ellis, ma'am," Tara said, the image of politeness.

Rex shook his head. This lady never ceased to amaze him with her constant transformations.

Grandma Grayson exchanged glances with Grandma Helen. Rex could see the gears turning in their minds. This wasn't good.

"And what do you do, Miss Ellis?" Grandma Helen asked.

"I'm a radiologist," she replied.

*Huh, a doctor.* Who would have thought? Her bedside manners—from what he'd experienced at the airport—seemed quite lacking.

"A doctor?" Grandma Grayson said. "I've always wanted one of those in my family."

Rex's pulse shot up. This wasn't happening. One of them might get engaged at this rate if care wasn't taken. And it couldn't be him. It was time to disappear.

"Grandma, I need to head to the hotel," Rex interjected.

"Why?" Grandma Grayson's face crinkled with concern. "Are you okay?"

"Just tired after the long flight. Grandma Helen, it was great to meet you."

"Me too, young man," Grandma Helen said with

a knowing smile. It was as if she'd guessed he was running away. "I hope we get a chance to chat some other time."

"I hope so too, ma'am. Have a good day, and congratulations again." He caught Dex's eye and gestured in the direction of the main entrance.

Then he gave everyone a small wave and strode through the room into the foyer until he'd exited the French doors.

He took a deep breath and exhaled, then loosened his tie. Thank goodness that was over. His emotions were still all over the place from meeting his family, and he needed time to process everything.

The door opened then closed behind him.

"You ran out of there like your tail was set on fire," Dex drawled.

Rex turned to see him leaning against the wall. "You wouldn't if you were me?"

Dex chuckled. "Well, those two together do look formidable."

Rex moved until he stood beside Dex. "You don't know the half of it. There's a reason Grandma Grayson is known as the Iron Lady."

Dex gave him a quick glance. "Iron Lady?"

"Anything she wants done gets done. I mean

anything. It was time to disappear before she got any ideas."

"Like you and Tara?"

"Hey! What do you mean?"

"You think I can't sense what's going on between you two?"

Rex ran a hand through his hair. Dex had to be kidding. "There's nothing between us. She's just a stranger I met today."

"That's how it usually starts."

Dex hadn't seen her behavior at the airport. "Not in this case." Then he remembered the kiss, and his heart raced. *No way!* He couldn't let his mind go there. There could *never* be anything between them, especially with her questionable character.

"Anyway, don't close your mind to it. You never know."

Rex didn't need this discussion. It was time to explain why he'd called Dex out, but first he had to know something else. "How's Maggie? I noticed she didn't come with you guys." Maggie had been his ma's best friend and had stayed to raise him and his brothers after their ma died. She was like a second mom.

"She was here earlier but had to leave for her second honeymoon," Dex replied.

Rex froze. "Maggie got married?"

"Yep! Her husband is a well-known New York general surgeon, and her former sweetheart. But don't worry, he's retired now, and they have a home on the ranch. Really nice guy, and he adores her."

Rex shook his head in wonder. "Who would have thought? But she deserves it one hundred percent after all the grief you guys gave her growing up."

Dex jabbed Rex's shoulder. "As if you didn't contribute. She's always missed you, and though she never said it, she must have felt like she let Ma down."

"I've missed her too. And her chocolate cookies. Hers were always out of this world."

"I'm sure she'll be happy to know you're back."

"I'd like to be the one to tell her."

"Okay. I'll let everyone know you said that."

"Thanks. So I'm going to be in Dexington for a few days, then come to the ranch."

"For good?" Dex's face was hopeful, and Rex hated that he had to disappoint him. Everything depended on whether Rex and his partners found the property they wanted.

"I'm not sure yet," Rex said. "But I'd like to spend some time with you guys."

Dex smiled. "That would be great. We've missed you so much, and we need to catch up."

"And we still have a lot to discuss." Like Tammy.

Dex placed his arm over Rex's shoulders. "We'll take it one step at a time. We can talk about it whenever you're ready. Whatever happened won't change the fact that we want you home."

Rex felt a knot ease in his heart. "Thank you."

Dex locked eyes with him. "You're family, bro. We love you and that's never gonna change, okay?"

And Rex wanted to believe it with everything in him. "Okay."

Dex patted his shoulder. "Good." Then he straightened. "I need to go back in there. What's your number?"

Rex rattled out the number to him.

"Okay. I'll call you."

"You don't need to write it down?"

"I'll remember. I hope you still know the way home."

Rex punched Dex's shoulder. "Like I'll ever forget."

Dex winced and rubbed his arm. "You pack a punch. What have you been eating and doing out there?"

Rex chuckled. "Same as you. I'll talk to you later."

"Alright. See you soon." Dex headed back in, waving before shutting the door behind him.

Rex straightened. He had to get a move on. Though there was a lot that still needed to be aired and resolved with his family, Rex was glad he'd finally seen them again. And now he could look forward to going home to the ranch and spending time with them.

Then he remembered Tara and grimaced. Since she was Dex's fiancée's friend, there was a chance she might end up at the ranch as well.

But Rex hoped that wouldn't be the case.

The last thing he needed was a drama queen witnessing his vulnerable, already complicated family situation.

# CHAPTER 13

Rex looked up from the file of papers he'd been working on as Weston, Liam, and Cole entered his hotel room. The guys had reserved the penthouse floor, which had enough bedrooms for all of them, but Rex had opted to stay one floor below. He'd needed the space and privacy to prepare himself to meet his family—which was a moot point now.

"I'm tuckered out," Weston said, flopping on the bed and stretching out.

"Me too," Cole said and settled on the couch in the room.

"You missed out," Liam said as he grabbed the only visitor's chair in the space.

"What did I miss?" Rex asked. He closed the file on the desk, got up, and moved over to the couch.

"All the matchmaking the grandmas were up to," Cole replied.

Thank goodness for that. He'd dodged a bullet.

Weston sat up and shot Rex an accusing glare. "How could you run off and leave us behind to deal with them?"

Rex chuckled. "You guys were up to it. Besides, no one asked you to stay rooted on the spot."

"We had no choice," Cole said. "Grandma would have killed us if we tried. Tara and Zoey disappeared right after you left. But it was nice to meet your family. I can't wait until we get all the juicy stories from them about your younger self."

Rex grabbed a throw pillow and hurled it at Cole's head.

Cole dodged the pillow. "Hey! What was that for?"

"A warning," Rex said. "This is one situation where you should bridle your tongue." Cole glared at him.

"So what did you think of Tara?" Weston asked. He'd laid back down. Rex gave him a suspicious glance. "Just asking."

"Yeah, right," Rex said. "I can smell your horse-poop from a mile away."

"She's pretty," Liam said.

"Looks ain't everything," Rex said.

"So you agree she's pretty," Weston said with a knowing smile.

"It doesn't matter what I think."

Weston's eyebrows lifted. "Are you sure about that? Dex let it slip that there might be something between you two."

*That babble mouth.* Rex would deal with him later.

"And of course, Tara denied it," Cole said. "Though she might have been blushing a bit while doing so."

*Blushing?* There was no way Tara would have been blushing unless she was thinking about…

"And now your ears are red too," Cole stated matter-of-factly.

Rex threw another pillow at him, and this time it hit Cole smack on the head.

"Ouch! That hurts," Cole protested.

Could it be the kiss had affected her too? Still, it didn't change anything. Rex wasn't interested, and she wasn't his type.

"Earth to Rex," Weston said.

"What?"

"You zoned out there for a minute."

"Maybe he's thinking about Tara," Cole said.

"You know what I think?" Rex said. "I think you need more than a pillow to get your head straightened."

Cole held up his hands in surrender. "I'm sorry."

Weston laughed. "Nice way to weasel out of a head smacking."

"I think Tara's cool," Liam said quietly.

Rex scoffed. "You don't know her."

"And you do? Did something bad happen between you two?" Weston asked, his eyes alive with curiosity.

Rex almost told them what happened at the airport—minus the kiss—but decided it was a story best left untold. It would do Tara no favors.

"I still think she's nice," Liam said stubbornly.

Rex studied Liam's face. Had he developed a crush on Tara? Rex had to admit it didn't really sit well with him. But why? Tara meant nothing to him. But more than that, there was no way he would wish the young lady on one of his best friends—she would walk all over him.

But there was no need to put the cart before the horse

—Liam hadn't even said he liked her. Best to leave the Tara topic alone. "I read the email you sent this morning, Weston." Weston had received news about a large tract of land that had just come up for sale in Dexin.

Weston sat up. "You saw that? So what do you think?"

"If I recall, that's some prime land, but I'll have to see it before I can make a final judgement. When would they be able to give us a tour?"

"In two days."

Rex thought for a moment. He could rest tomorrow and then see his family first the day after next. "That works for me." He glanced around the room. "What about you guys?"

"I'm in," Cole said.

"It's fine," Liam said.

"Great," Weston said. "I'm assuming you'll be back with your family by then, right?" Rex nodded. "So why don't we meet at the property at ten a.m. on Tuesday and go to your place once we're done there?"

"Sounds like a plan," Rex said.

"Awesome."

"So what's on your agenda for the rest of the day?"

"A shower, sightseeing, and then dinner," Weston said. "Planning to join us?"

"Not this time. I need more sleep."

"Alright. We'll get out of your way. Come on, boys."

"I'm only a year younger than you," Liam protested, but he still rose to his feet and followed them out.

Rex laid his head back on the couch.

Two more days, and then he'd be back at the ranch.

"Wow! This place is beautiful!" Tara exclaimed as she looked around the main house at Dexin Ranch. They'd spent the rest of Saturday with the Dexingtons and had even gone to church with them on Sunday for a thanksgiving service, then taken a tour bus around the city for a bit of sightseeing. It'd been so much fun, and Grandma Helen had been a hoot. Now they'd arrived back at the ranch, and even though Tara was exhausted, the excursion had been worth it.

She hadn't known what to expect at the ranch, but she hadn't been prepared for the beautiful architecture of the log-and-stone home she'd just stepped into. Every furnishing in the space had either a log or stone element, and both had been blended seamlessly to create a rustic yet modern masterpiece that was warm and inviting.

"Isn't it? Max's mom created this place with the boys," Becca said, leading the way into the living room. They'd come in via a side entrance and then through the mudroom where they'd dropped off their boots—Tara was glad she had remembered to bring a pair along for the trip. Dex and Jax were unloading the car, while Max had carried a sleeping Chloe ahead of them into the house. "Please take a seat." She gestured to the large couch in the space.

"Thank you," Tara said as she settled in. Then she noticed Zoey was staring at her phone with a disappointed look on her face. "What is it, Zoey?"

"It's Miss Prissy. She tried to reach me earlier and then sent me a message that your booking at her bed and breakfast didn't work out. There was some kind of mix-up."

Tara's face fell. Zoey had gushed so much about how quaint the bed and breakfast place, and Tara had been looking forward to a soak in its vintage bathtub. Talk about a weekend of mix-ups. She couldn't wait for it to be over.

Then Zoey's face brightened. "But it's not a big deal," she said. "You can share my room with me. It'll be like old times."

"Why don't you stay with us?" Becca said. "We have enough room, and the second floor is practically empty."

"I wouldn't want to intrude," Tara said, though the idea did appeal to her. She'd never stayed at a ranch, and she'd wanted to a very long time ago.

"It's absolutely fine," Becca said. "We'd love to have you."

"I'm not sure—"

"Thanks for the offer," Zoey interjected. "She'll take it."

"Hey!" Tara whispered.

"Awesome!" Becca said with a smile. "I'll get your room ready for you."

"Thank you," Tara said, caving in.

"I'll be back shortly." Becca strode up the long winding staircase that led to the second floor and soon disappeared from view.

Tara narrowed her eyes at Zoey. "What are you up to? I could have stayed with you."

Zoey plopped down beside her on the couch. "Here's much better, and you'll have your own room and privacy. Besides, I'm looking out for my friend."

Tara stared at her in confusion. "What do you mean?"

"You'll see," Zoey replied with a mischievous smile.

Tara studied Zoey's face. She'd seen that look before. It was her up-to-no-good smile. Could it be …? She grabbed Zoey's arm as comprehension dawned. "Are you serious right now?"

Zoey chuckled and extricated her arm from Tara's grip. "You need all the help you can get. Don't worry, you won't be sleeping in the same house as him. Rex has his own place."

"I'm going to kill you."

Zoey laughed. "As if that's possible. You love me too much to do it."

Tara collapsed back on the couch. How was she going to survive being on the same property with Rex?

She had a feeling they'd strangle each other before the trip was over.

# CHAPTER 15

Rex took a deep inhale as he stepped down from his SUV, which he'd parked in front of the main house. The refreshing early morning air mixed with the sweet smell of hay and honeysuckle and the faint scent of horseflesh filled his nostrils.

He'd missed this place—God's own heaven on earth with its kaleidoscope of gorgeous colors from the flowering meadows that stretched out as far as the eyes could see, and the towering, majestic mountains in the background with streams running like silver through them. There was truly nowhere like home.

Rex had arrived very early at the ranch so as to help out with the morning chores. Just the few days he'd spent in Dexington away from horses had him missing them already. He'd settle in later once that was done. Rex still had a key to the house, so he let himself in through the side entrance and pulled off his boots in the mudroom. Except for the new boots and coats stored there, the space still appeared the same, like he'd never left.

As he exited the mudroom, someone stepped on his foot.

*Ouch!* Rex staggered back, his toes hurting like they'd been attacked by bees. Who was this person that couldn't watch where they were going? As he rubbed his foot, he glanced up.

Tara.

Rex groaned. Not her again—though he had to admit she looked fantastic in the form-fitting workout clothes she wore. What was she doing here this early in the day? Rex hoped it didn't mean she was staying at the house. He loved his peace and quiet and didn't care to butt heads with her during his stay.

"I'm sorry," she said. "I wasn't watching where I was going."

Rex's eyes widened. This was a first. Tara was apologizing? She hadn't seemed like the type that did so.

Then her face blanched and settled into a mask, as if she suddenly realized who she'd been talking to. "Oh, it's you."

What did that mean? That she wouldn't have apologized if she'd known it was him? "What are you doing here?" he asked.

"Why? I shouldn't be here?"

"That's not what I meant. Just surprised to see you here, that's all."

"I have to go." She brushed past him and continued out of the house.

Rex watched her leave. What was up with her anyway? He didn't understand her. He tested his foot and realized it didn't hurt as much anymore. Rex continued into the house and headed straight to the kitchen, where he was more likely to find someone awake. Becca was mixing something in a bowl on the kitchen island and looked up as he entered.

"Good morning," she called out cheerfully. "I'm glad you made it."

"Good morning, Becca," he said. "Just here to grab some coffee and I'll get out of your way."

She gestured to the coffee maker. "There's coffee in the machine for anyone who wants. Feel free to grab a cup and come chat with me."

"Thanks." Rex retrieved a mug from the cupboard, rinsed it, and poured himself some. Then he settled in on one of the kitchen stools on the other side of the island. He took a sip of the coffee. Black and hot just the way he liked it.

"You and your brothers are the same," Becca said. "How can you drink coffee without some milk or sugar?"

"Ma and Pa loved it this way. We ended up picking up the same habits." He took another sip of his coffee. "So how are you?" he asked. "Congratulations again on the baby."

Becca beamed. "Thank you. Sometimes I still can't believe it. I didn't think I'd get pregnant again, since Max and I are already in our forties, and I was satisfied with just Chloe. But I'm happy about him."

Rex sipped his coffee. "Is it going to be a boy?"

"We don't know yet. But it's what I feel in my heart. Mother's intuition."

"Anything I can do to help? To make things easier for you?"

"Really? I do have one request."

"What?"

"Could you stop Max and your brothers from hovering over me? They're worse than mother hens!"

Rex chuckled. "Sorry, can't help you there. It was ingrained into us by our ma."

Becca gave him an amused smile. "And I assume you're only going to make it worse."

"My apologies in advance for that."

Becca let out an exaggerated sigh. "Oh well, what's one more hen?"

Rex laughed. He liked Becca. "Are you always this funny?"

"I aim to please."

Rex drained his coffee and then washed the mug before placing it on the rack to dry. "I enjoyed this time with you, but I need to go take care of the horses."

"Still the horse whisperer—already missing the horses like crazy?" a familiar voice said. Rex turned to see Dex leaning against the wall. He hadn't heard him come in.

"It's been a few days."

"I understand the feeling. You're welcome to take over the horse chores."

"Don't you need to go check out your new place?" Becca asked.

"My place?" Rex gave Dex a questioning look.

"We had your place built out like we'd always talked about," Dex said.

"But how? I know we had our inheritance, but I'd taken my share. Even then, it wouldn't have been enough for the place."

"Max built it for you. Your brother is quite the rich man." Becca snorted. "Okay, a billionaire."

Rex gave her a disbelieving look. Max had taken his inheritance and invested it immediately through a college friend of his. But a billionaire? Good for him.

"Anyway, you have a place of your own on the plot you chose years ago, and I already cleaned it up last night," Dex said. "The key is under the flowerpot by the entrance."

"Thank you," Rex said. He had a place of his own. This was good news, especially since it meant he didn't have to sleep under the same roof as Tara. Crisis averted.

"My pleasure," Dex replied. "So I'm happy to leave the horses in the main barn to you. It's still in the same place, though the barn has been updated. The ranch hands will take care of the other horses at the second barn."

Rex straightened. It seemed nothing much had changed about the chore distribution. "I should get going before the day breaks. Thanks again for the coffee, Becca." He headed toward the exit.

"Wait!" Becca said. Rex turned to face her. "Can Tara go with you?"

"Why?" Rex said. "She'll only be in the way."

"I heard that." Tara strode into view, still decked out in her workout outfit. "Why do I have to go with *him*?"

"It'll be fun," Becca said, her eyes twinkling.

"I'd prefer to go to the gym while it's still early."

Rex gave a disbelieving chuckle. "There's no gym here."

"How do you know? You just got here."

"There's no gym," Dex said quietly.

"Of course there isn't," Rex said matter-of-factly. "There's enough chores on a ranch for a good workout."

"Which is why taking care of the horses with Rex would be good for you," Becca said good-naturedly.

"Can't I work with Dex instead?"

"Sorry, Tara, but I already passed the buck to Rex," Dex replied.

Rex bristled. She was refusing so sharply, but who ever said Rex wanted to work with her? Most horses were gentle, but he didn't need a newbie like her getting underfoot and causing problems. "I'm not sure—"

"Oh come on, Rex. Tara hasn't been in a true

horse barn, and I'm sure you'll be the absolute gentleman and keep her safe," Becca said as if reading his mind. "Now, both of you, enough of the excuses. Just go!"

"Hold on," a familiar voice said.

# CHAPTER 16

Rex turned to see Max enter the kitchen. "Good morning," he said. His brother looked great as usual in his business suit.

"Morning," Max replied with a grin. "Glad you made it here early."

"I thought you'd left for work," Becca said.

"I did leave, dear, but then I saw an unknown SUV parked outside in Rex's favorite spot, and I assumed he'd arrived. I came back since I know he can't stay away from the horses, which means he needs to comply with this new requirement we have on the ranch. I'm sure we can handle it quickly, and then I'll be off again. Tara, Rex, could you please follow me?"

What could it be? Rex looked at Dex, who only shrugged.

"Do you know what it is?" Tara asked quietly as they followed Max past the double French doors and down the hallway to what Rex remembered was his office.

"No idea," Rex said.

"I guess you're just as clueless as I am."

Rex bristled at her words. She was certainly living up to his expectations that she would be rude.

They reached Max's office and stepped in.

The place looked different than Rex remembered. Floor-to-ceiling bookshelves—filled with what Rex assumed to be medical texts—now lined one-half of the walls. A massive desk and a custom swivel chair occupied a spot near the large windows, while a large black leather sofa with its own coffee table rested against one wall.

"You may sit," Max said, gesturing to the couch. Rex and Tara sat at opposite ends.

Max leaned against the desk and faced them.

"What's going on?" Rex asked.

"Rex, are you sick, or do you have a fever?"

"No. I'm healthier than a horse. Why?"

"When was your last tetanus shot?"

Rex thought for a moment. Frankly, he couldn't

remember, though he was sure he'd received one a couple of years ago. Rex hated jabs of any kind, so he tended to be extra careful when working on the ranch.

"I thought that would be the case," Max said. "So I'd like you to get one before you start any chores today."

Rex's pulse quickened. Why hadn't he arrived when he was sure Max had gone to work? Rex could take stitches any day without even flinching, but shots? The mere thought of them gave him hives.

"And I'd like Dr. Ellis here to give it to you," Max continued. "And before you ask, she's required by the hospital she works at to be current on hers."

Rex froze. Max had to be joking. "Why can't *you* give me the shot?" His brother was an emergency doctor and had given him injections in the past.

Max's eyebrow rose. "Is there a reason why Dr. Ellis can't administer it?"

Rex had always hated it when Max went into doctor mode. "You can't be serious. She's a radiologist, for goodness sake." Rex didn't work in the medical field, but weren't radiologists the ones who did X-rays and MRIs? What did they have to do with shots?

Tara scoffed. "I'm a qualified MD first, and

doctors can give injections," she shot back. "Besides, I'm board-certified in both internal medicine and radiology, so I'm doubly qualified, cowboy." She gave him a curious look. "Or are you one of those people who's a big baby when it comes to needles?"

"Of course not!" he protested. Though he totally was.

"Then it shouldn't be a problem, right, cowboy?"

"Or you could drive all the way to Dexington to get it," Max said. "But I can't let you near the horses until you do. It's your choice."

Why hadn't they mentioned it when he'd seen them in Dexington? He couldn't go back there now. Max had checkmated him, and he knew it.

Max straightened, then gestured to the stainless-steel kidney tray, surgical gloves, and sanitizer on his desk. Rex had seen enough of them during Tammy's cancer treatments to know what they were. "I've prepared what you need, Dr. Ellis."

Tara rose and made her way to the desk. "Thanks, Dr. Dexin," she said. "Don't worry, cowboy, this will be quick," she said to Rex. "I'll need you to remove your shirt."

Rex said nothing and took off his checkered shirt to reveal the sleeveless black T-shirt he'd worn beneath.

Tara squirted some sanitizer into her hands and rubbed them together. Then she donned the surgical gloves, grabbed the tray, and headed back in his direction.

Rex watched with trepidation as she placed the tray on the coffee table, picked up the injection ampoule, broke its cap, and drained its contents with a syringe and needle, making sure to remove air bubbles from the syringe. Then she replaced the needle with a new one and uncapped it.

He swallowed as she swabbed a small area of his upper arm with an alcohol wipe in her left hand and then squeezed the muscle. This couldn't be happening.

"I don't think he's ready, Dr. Dexin," Tara said, wiggling the needle for effect.

Rex broke out in a sweat. "Wait. What do you mean? I—"

He felt a quick jab into his arm, but before he could pull away, Tara was massaging the area with a cotton swab, placing a band-aid over it, and patting his arm. "You're all set, cowboy."

It was over? She'd distracted him just to get the shot in? Rex was surprised how quick and almost painless it had been.

"Thanks, Dr. Ellis," Max said as she capped the needle and returned it to the tray.

"You're welcome." She removed the gloves and dumped them on the tray as well.

"Rex, I'll make a note of this on your immunization record here," Max said. "Let me know if you'll like me to send a copy to your PCP." The PCP was Rex's primary physician. "That wasn't so bad now, was it?"

# CHAPTER 17

Tara followed Rex into the horse barn and down the cobblestone aisle. She'd been surprised when Max had asked her to administer the shot, and it'd been interesting to see how much Rex hated needles, but he'd ended up taking it like a champ. Now she wondered how her experience here would be with the roles reversed.

The place was much larger and more modern than she'd expected, with rows upon rows of horse stalls made of wood and metal, most of which appeared occupied. There was a hay loft on the second level packed high with hay bales. But the barn was much cleaner than she'd expected. The air was thick with the smell of sweet hay, leather, and pine, but Tara didn't find it unpleasant. She'd never really been around animals growing up, so she wasn't sure how she'd feel around these horses.

Some of the horses trotted forward and stuck their heads out beyond their stalls, and Tara watched as Rex reached out, rubbed their necks, patted them, and even offered them treats. The horses nuzzled him in return, and he chuckled. It was like seeing another side of him, and she couldn't believe he could be this gentle. But how was that even possible? From what she'd understood from Zoey, Rex had lost contact with his family for many years, so chances were he'd never met these specific horses before. Yet here they were, cozying up to him. How was he able to win them over so quickly?

Then he headed to a room at the back of the barn and soon returned with two sets of gloves and a wheelbarrow which held two manure forks. "We need to muck out their stalls. We can start out at this end and work down. Here," he said, holding out a pair of gloves and one of the forks to her.

Tara swallowed. If she understood what he was saying, she had to enter the stalls where the horses were. Tara had nothing against animals, but couldn't he see that these horses were huge? Zoey once told her how her mom had died after being kicked by a horse. What if that happened to her? She had no experience dealing with such powerful animals.

Rex must have sensed her trepidation. "Have you ever done this before?"

She shook her head. She hated being this vulnerable. Tara had sworn to herself that she'd never be weak, but here she was afraid of some horses.

"Okay," he said softly. "Have you ever been near a horse?"

Tara shook her head again. There was no sense in hiding it.

"Why don't I introduce you to one of the horses who I think is gentler, and then we'll go from there? Can you do that?"

"Yes."

"Great." He dropped the fork in the wheelbarrow and the gloves into his back pocket and led her to one of the larger stalls at the end. A beautiful dark horse ambled forward and poked its head out of the stall. "Just some things to keep in mind," Rex said. "Horses are like big babies, and they're sensitive to how we react to them. You have to be careful not to startle them with any sudden movements, but you don't have to be afraid of them either. They're the nicest creatures in the world."

Tara believed him, but that didn't mean she still

wasn't afraid. But maybe it was like her martial arts instructor had said: *To know your enemy, you have to discover his strengths and weaknesses.* Maybe she just needed to apply the same principle here.

"And never stand right behind them," Rex finished. "Does that make sense?"

"Sure." She'd understood everything he'd said, but putting his suggestions into practice was another thing altogether. Yet she couldn't let him see her fear. Tara could do this.

"Good." Rex turned back to the horse and rubbed her neck. "Hello, beautiful."

"She's a girl?" Tara asked.

"Yes."

"What's her name?"

"I don't know that yet. I just got back."

"But you seem familiar with her, with all of them."

"I'm good with horses. Been around them all my life." Then he patted the mare's neck, pulled out a small brown bag from his pocket, and offered it to Tara. "Do you want to try giving her a treat?"

Tara accepted the bag. "Sure, but how do I do that?" She didn't want to make a mistake.

"Just take one of the treats from the bag and put it in the flat of your hand. And then offer it to her. Let me show you." He took a treat from the bag and presented it to the horse. Tara watched, then she tried the same, her heart in her mouth.

The mare accepted the offering and then nuzzled her hand. Her lips felt both soft and hard at the same time. Tara wished the horse would do it again.

"Now rub her side like this." Rex demonstrated, and Tara mimicked his actions. The mare's coat was smoother than silk. Tara couldn't help touching it over and over again.

"Okay, now stroke her neck," he said, and Tara obeyed. "See how she likes that?"

The horse had moved closer to her and was now nuzzling her chest.

Tara chuckled. What was this horse thinking? Rex must have noticed it too, because his face turned red.

*Oooh, that's interesting.* She'd never have pegged Rex for the blushing type. But he was probably getting more embarrassed by the minute, so Tara adjusted until the mare was nuzzling her neck.

"She likes you," he said after a while.

Tara thought so too. "Thanks," she said after a while.

"For what?"

"For taking the time to teach me. For not calling me a wuss for being afraid."

"Why would I? It's natural if you've never been around horses."

"Not everyone would feel the same." Tara had a few ideas from her previous experiences on the sort of people who would make fun of her.

"Then such folks are not worth knowing," he stated.

Tara stared at him in surprise. She would never have imagined that Rex would take her side. Had she misjudged him?

"Okay, why don't you give the horses their treats, and I'll do the mucking?" Rex said. "Does that work?"

Tara's shoulders relaxed. Truthfully, she wasn't yet ready to dive into the world of poop disposal, not when she still felt this nervous around horses. "Sounds good."

"Okay, give me one second." Rex retreated back into the room with one fork and returned with a much bigger brown bag. He passed it to her. "Their treats."

"Thanks."

"You're welcome." Rex moved the wheelbarrow as close as he could to the stall opposite the mare's and started from there. Tara watched as he mucked out the first stall and then filled it with fresh hay that was stacked on a wooden platform in the corner of the barn. Now she knew what to do if it ever came to it. Then she turned back to feed the mare, who was more than happy to accept another treat.

They worked that way down the stalls, Tara petting and feeding the horses and Rex freshening their quarters. Soon they reached the end of the line.

"I'll be right back," Rex said. He left the barn with the fork on top of the full wheelbarrow and came back a few minutes later with an empty one with a clean fork in it, both of which he returned to the room at the other end.

"There's one more thing to take care of," he said. "I'll need to send down some bales of hay from the loft to replace the hay we've used."

"Let me help," Tara said. This one she could easily do.

He shook his head. "I can do it alone. It'll only take a few minutes."

"I can help," Tara insisted. "I'd like to."

He studied her for a moment and then nodded. "Alright." He grabbed the second set of gloves from his back pocket and handed them to her.

Tara donned them as Rex led her up the stairs to the loft. The area was piled high with stacks and stacks of hay. Tara guessed there might be over a thousand bales in the space. He moved to an area marked out with red paint. "We'll stack six bales here in this spot."

"Why there?" Tara asked.

"That's where the hay elevator is. We'll send it down once we're done."

"So you don't have to carry each bale down? Smart."

Rex lifted a bale from a stack and carried it to the spot. Tara did the same and the straightened to see Rex studying her. "I didn't think you'd be strong enough to carry it."

"I like surprising people," Tara said.

"Consider me surprised. There's hope for you yet," he said with a smirk.

Tara liked this side of Rex. Goodness the guy was cute, in a manly sort of way. "You're an ass, you know that right?" Tara teased back.

Rex chuckled. "You're the first to call me that."

"I can assure you others have been blind."

Rex laughed, the sound sending the kind of delicious electricity Tara wouldn't mind experiencing over and over again down her spine. There was something about a good laugh that did things to Tara's insides. If she wasn't careful, she'd fall for this guy.

She turned back to carry another bale, and soon all six bales were stacked in the center. Then Rex pressed a switch on the wall, and the square platform with the bales descended through the floor, then stopped once it reached the ground. Tara followed Rex down the stairs and began helping move the bales to the corner. Then Rex pressed another switch on the ground level, and the platform returned back to the second floor.

"Why don't we wash our hands and then we can leave?" Rex led her to the room at the back, which he informed her was called the tack room. There were two farmhouse sinks in the medium-sized utilitarian space, and they both stood side-by-side to wash their hands after disposing their gloves in a metal container.

Their shoulders brushed together, and Tara felt a spark of electricity buzz through her. But it seemed she was the only one, since Rex didn't react and just continued to wash his hands before rinsing off and drying them. Why was she having all these strange bodily reactions to him?

With her mind still trying to decipher what was going on, Rex led her all the way to the barn's entrance. By now dawn had arrived, and the sun could be seen making its way out.

"That's it for now," Rex said. "Thanks for helping."

"You're welcome, but I didn't do much," Tara replied. She'd had a good time—nothing like the tension-filled awkward atmosphere she'd been expecting—and thankfully, Rex had been a gentleman and hadn't held the injection shot against her.

"I guess I'll see you later," he said as he locked the barn behind them.

"Have a good day," Tara called out as she made her way back to the main house.

She wished the same peaceful day for herself, but she wasn't sure her mind would stop trying to understand why Rex affected her so.

Rex stood beside the SUV and surveyed the house in front of him. It was a large, single-level home made of stone and log just like the main house but with an attached garage. Flower hedges lined the entrance instead of a full-blown garden like the one he'd seen at Dex's. Rex was glad for it—he definitely had no green thumb.

He grabbed his luggage and headed to the main door. Rex found the flowerpot like Dex had described and lifted it to retrieve the key there. Then he inserted it into the keyhole and pushed the door open.

A smile lit up his face as he closed the door behind him. The spacious interior boasted various shades of the greys and browns he favored with an occasional burnt orange furnishing. Dex had done a great job cleaning the space, and it looked airy and pristine.

Rex headed toward the gourmet kitchen, which featured a large granite countertop that contrasted nicely with the dark cabinets. The guys must have been thinking about his future family when they'd installed the kitchen, because Rex only cooked when he had to. He didn't love cooking like Dex did, so for now, Rex planned to stick to eating his meals at the main house.

But then he noticed the one thing he'd ever want in a kitchen, sitting against the backsplash.

A French press.

Rex grinned as he reached for it. He was a coffee snob, had always been. And his brothers hadn't forgotten. He checked the cabinet right under it. Like he'd hoped, there was a fresh bag of Ethiopian coffee beans.

Ah, his brothers had done him good.

He turned and checked out the rest of the house. There was a large master bedroom with a walk-in closet, two other guest rooms, a laundry room, and a study with a large couch, custom-made desks with chairs on either end, and massive floor-to-ceiling bookshelves. Then there was the sunroom which had a view of the mountains. It was a large, spacious area he could turn into whatever he wanted. Rex returned to the living room and then headed to a side door he'd noticed tucked into the back. He opened it and stepped through.

A large workspace that could accommodate three cars side by side greeted him. And it was a restorer's dream with its LED ceiling lights and a whole back section filled with all the high-end mechanic's tools and supplies he'd ever need. Next to horses, there was nothing Rex loved more than classic cars. There was something beautiful about them he couldn't resist. He'd stopped his amateur wrenching after moving to Texas, but he'd never forgotten the hobby and had always bought the latest car magazines and attended classic car shows whenever he could.

But the highlight of the garage was the red 1951 Ford F1 pickup he'd been working on for years and never finished restoring before he left. It was parked in the center spot with a vehicle cover over it. Rex resisted the urge to whip the cover off—he'd never leave it alone for the rest of the day if he did, and he still needed to settle in.

Rex made his way back to the living room. The house was more than he'd expected.

And it was his space.

Even though he'd had his own home in Texas, it

had been more like a place to sleep and eat and nothing else.

But this house reflected who he was, the person that had been buried under the numerous hospital visits and then subsequent death of Tammy. The *him* he was looking forward to getting reacquainted with again. Rex had lost so much, and he hadn't even known it.

He carried his luggage into the master bedroom, placed the cylindrical bag in a safe spot, unpacked, took a shower, and then changed into a fresh pair of jeans and a T-shirt. He would spend the rest of the day getting to know his new place.

But then he remembered his morning with Tara at the barn. He hadn't expected to see her let down her guard and be so open with him about her unfamiliarity with horses. And he hadn't minded that side of her. In fact, he'd preferred it—he could tell it was a more honest representation of her than he'd ever seen. He'd been happy to help her, and she hadn't minded his presence. In fact, she'd even teased him at the end, which he'd found refreshing.

Yet he'd been surprised at how strong she was. Rex hadn't imagined the slim beauty would be able to lift bales of hay like it was nothing. To be frank, he'd found it attractive.

And then their shoulders had touched. He'd pretended as if nothing had happened, but his heart had been galloping like it wanted to fly out of his chest, which was an intense feeling he'd never felt before.

But what did that mean? Was he attracted to Tara? Rex wasn't sure. Then he remembered their first encounter, and he mentally shook his head.

There was no way he was attracted to Tara. If she was the kind of person he'd first met at the rental counter, it would only mean heartbreak for him at the end—not that he was looking for a relationship.

And that was a risk Rex wasn't ready to take.

# CHAPTER 19

Tara piled her dish high with food from the spread that covered the dinner table: buttermilk chicken that looked so tender Tara was sure it would melt in her mouth, cheesy fried bean casserole with a touch of garlic and jalapeños, sweet tangy meatballs, spicy baby back ribs, and mixed salads.

Dessert was a triple chocolate tiramisu that Tara couldn't seem to get enough of. By the time she was done, Tara wasn't sure how much longer her jeans button would hold up before bursting open. Fortunately, she had a high metabolism, and she wasn't ashamed to make the most of it.

"How was the food?" Becca asked.

"Very delicious, thank you."

"Oh she enjoyed it alright," Zoey teased. She'd joined them for dinner along with Rex, Jax, and Dex. It turned out eating meals together was a Dexin family ritual.

"I did, and I'm not ashamed to admit it," Tara stated. "Good food should be appreciated, and the best way to do so is by actually eating it. Thanks for the wonderful meal."

"Oh, it's not me you should thank," Becca said. "Dex was the one who cooked dinner."

"Really?" Tara said. "Now, why are you taken?" she teased.

Dex chuckled. "Sorry about that." He leaned forward. "But we do have others available who would do just fine."

*Oh no!* Tara had been trying to avoid any form of matchmaking, and now she'd just stepped into it. Talk about shooting herself in the foot.

"Count me out," Jax stated. "Just the idea of having a wife makes me run in the opposite direction."

"That's because you've not met the right woman," Max stated and gave his wife a kiss on the cheek. He turned to Chloe and did the same, then rose to his feet. "I have to go take care of work. I'll see you guys later."

"Goodnight, Daddy," Chloe said.

"Don't worry, darling. Daddy will still come and read you your bedtime story."

Chloe beamed. "Alright." It was clear she adored her father. Soon he'd disappeared out of view.

Tara loved the easy camaraderie between Max and Becca. If marriage were for her, this would be the kind of relationship she'd want. But she didn't deserve a family, so that was never going to happen.

"So that leaves Rex," Becca said. "Not that we're trying to sell you off, Tara."

That was exactly what they were doing. But Tara knew it was all in good fun, so she just went along with it for now.

"Hmm," Dex said and leaned back as if putting on his thinking cap.

But Rex said nothing, and it seemed his mind was elsewhere. What could he be worrying about? And why was she suddenly noticing his chiseled jaw and the curve of those lips that triggered memories of the kiss they'd shared?

Then his eyes caught hers and held them. Tara felt her skin warm. The butterflies in her stomach fluttered as she stared into those twin pools of chocolate that would drown her in their warmth if she let them.

"Earth to Tara," Zoey said.

Tara returned to the present and noticed the rest of the table giving her knowing smiles.

Her cheeks warmed. How could she have allowed herself to get caught staring at Rex of all people? "You were saying something?" she managed to say.

"I'd love your help," Zoey said.

"You know I'll support you anytime."

"Promise?

"I promise."

"Awesome. So you'll help me co-chair a singles mixer event with Rex."

# CHAPTER 20

$\mathcal{R}$ex hadn't been listening in on the conversation around the dinner table. His mind was still preoccupied with his possible attraction to Tara. Watching her eat had only made it worse, since Rex loved a woman with a healthy appetite. So it had taken him a second to register that his name had been mentioned.

"What?" Maybe he hadn't heard properly.

"Remember Miss Prissy?" Dex asked.

Rex sure did. The woman loved her gossip, but she'd always been a good-natured soul.

"She's opened a matchmaking agency," Dex said. "And given how Zoey and I successfully got together, she reached out to us to co-chair a singles mixer event. Unfortunately, I'm super busy these days, and with Zoey starting at the ER center, it's next to impossible for us to handle it."

"What ER Center?" There was so much Rex was out of the loop on.

"Max built one in town, and it's opening in two weeks."

*An ER Center?* That was impressive, and Rex could guess Max had done it in memory of their ma, who hadn't been able to reach medical services on time before she'd passed. Max always promised he'd do something about it, and he'd finally made it come true.

"So I've volunteered Tara to take my place in planning the singles event," Zoey said.

"And you to take mine," Dex said.

Tara didn't seem pleased with the arrangement. "But—"

Zoey gave Tara a stern look. "You've already given your word," she said. Tara's shoulders slumped —she'd certainly tied herself up with that one. But it also showed she was the kind of person who kept her promises, which was always a good character trait to have. Not that she was important to him or anything.

"And you owe me, Rex," Dex said. "I've had to take on your responsibilities in addition to my own all these years. This is one way to start paying up.

Besides, you've always been good at organizing stuff."

Rex sighed. As much as he didn't care for this sort of event—considering all the gossip that would ensue with him back in town—he did owe Dex. The guy had been forced to handle the ranch operations singlehandedly after he skipped town.

But doing it with Tara? He was still trying to understand what was going on with his feelings. And now his family was fixing them up together—Rex could see the ruse for what it was—which would be like setting fire to kindling, and Rex had no plans to be burned. "I'm not sure that's a good idea," he said.

Dex leaned forward. "What I'm saying is you don't get a choice in the matter," he said with a twinkle in his eye. "Besides, it's only for a few weeks. I'm sure you can survive that."

"And it would be a great way to get reintegrated into Dexin society," Becca said.

Like he cared about that. Getting back into the community was hardly a priority for him—Rex had no time for the gossip that would spread from trying to do so. All he wanted was to enjoy getting to know his family again and maybe prep for his business' move to Dexin if it came to it. But it seemed his family had made up their mind, and he couldn't get out of the commitment. Good thing Tara seemed as vehemently opposed to the idea as he was—it would make it easier to get the planning for the event done on time, and then they could go their separate ways.

"I'm glad to see we all agree," Zoey said with glee when Rex made no further comment. "Thank you so much, Tara and Rex, for agreeing to do this. I'll have Miss Prissy call you whenever she's ready."

But all that discussion faded into the back of Rex's mind when he remembered the land he and the guys had to check out tomorrow.

If it didn't work out, would that be a sign that settling back in Dexin was never meant to be?

## CHAPTER 21

"Welcome to my home," Rex said as the guys piled into the living room after Rex had given them a tour of the space. They'd just returned from viewing the land they were interested in, and since it'd been much more than they'd expected—with existing permits for a horse breeding operation, very fertile land with lots of hay and alfalfa, and more than enough acreage to build out the operation as they desired—they'd made an offer on the spot.

The view of the land with its rolling hills had almost been as good as that of Dexin ranch, and it was a miracle that the place had been up for sale— the owners of the property had passed on, and their kids, who had moved to another state, weren't interested in returning. And though the ranch needed much work to make it more habitable, with several old buildings that had to be torn down, it had good bones and was well worth it. Rex could already see the horses running through the land in his mind. Now all they had to do was wait to hear back.

"Ah, I could live here," Cole said as he collapsed on the larger couch and put his feet up.

"This is really nice," Weston said, settling into a loveseat. "And your brothers built it? They must love you very much."

"Yes, he's one lucky man," Cole said. "I can't see you or Liam doing the same for me." Liam hurled a throw pillow at his head from where he sat on a smaller couch, and Cole managed to dodge it. "Hey, what was that for?"

"We might just decide to exclude you from the new ranch if you keep running your mouth," Liam said.

"You can't do that," Cole said with a smirk as he settled back into the couch. "Rex won't let you."

"So speaking of family," Weston said, "have you told them about Tammy?"

Rex sat on a couch arm. "Not yet."

"I know you, Rex," Liam said. "You won't be at peace until you do."

Rex ran a hand through his hair. "I know. I'll probably talk to them soon."

But how was he going to bring it up? And what if Max and his family got mad at him when they heard the details?

Still, he owed it to Tammy to tell them the truth.

Rex didn't have to think about that right now. "So are you guys staying for lunch?" he asked instead.

"I wish we could, but Grandma wants us back in Boston," Liam said. "She's keeping us on a tight leash now we're on the east coast. For now, we're going with the flow just to make her happy until we purchase the land."

"Hopefully they'll accept our offer, and we can proceed from there," Weston said. "Though we'll keep scouting for other real estate just in case this one falls through."

Then Cole straightened, reached out for something he'd caught sight of on the floor, and picked it up.

Rex grimaced. It was his old copy of *Oliver Twist*. It was as if coming back home had triggered other long-buried memories, and Rex had ended up picking up the book to read. He'd forgotten to put it away.

Cole raised an eyebrow. "You're reading this

book again? What is it about this book that you like so much?"

"Give me that," Rex said and snatched it away. "I just like it," he said and tucked it beside him.

"But why?"

"Cole, drop the topic," Liam said with a stern voice. Rex had never told them the history of the book, but Liam must have sensed that the subject was causing him distress.

"Okay," Cole said quietly as if chastised.

Weston rose to his feet. "Now, let's go say hi to your family before we leave."

# CHAPTER 22

Tara opened a bleary eye at the sound of her phone's ringtone and took in the beautiful pale blue and pink room that was hers for the duration of her stay at the ranch. She'd gotten up early in the morning while it was still dark to help Rex with the horses—and then returned to bed—as had become her habit since the first day they'd gone to the stable together, though they mostly worked in silence.

But it was like they'd come to a truce and were now comfortable around each other. Tara had become more familiar with the horses and even learned their names, but she hadn't worked up the courage to ask Rex to teach her how to ride them. But she hoped to one of these days. Still, she was enjoying her vacation so far.

She reached for her phone and swiped the answer button. "This is Tara Ellis."

"Hello, dear, this is Miss Prissy."

Tara sat up, all sleep fleeing from her eyes. "Good morning, ma'am."

"It's nice to hear your voice, dear," Miss Prissy said. "Zoey has talked so much about you."

"Thank you," Tara said.

"I believe Zoey has told you about the singles mixer event. We're so excited for that! Now, would you and Rex Dexin be able to come and see me at noon today? At the bed-and-breakfast?"

"That works for me, but I'll have to check in with Rex. I'm not sure what his schedule is like."

"Oh, I'm not worried about that. Just tell him it's Miss Prissy, his ma's old friend. I'm sure he'll make room," Miss Prissy said matter-of-factly.

Tara chuckled. "Okay, I'll tell him that."

"Great. So I'll see you both at noon. Tell him for me, will you?"

"I will."

"We'll have so much fun! Bye!" Miss Prissy ended the call.

Tara dropped her phone, and her head fell back on her pillow. She snickered as she thought about what Miss Prissy had said. She wasn't sure how much fun Rex could have with Miss Prissy, but regardless it would be a sight to behold. This would make her day if it happened.

But first she had to inform the guy in question.

Tara didn't have his phone number, which meant she had to tell him in person, and better now than later in case he needed to rearrange his plans. She'd never been to his new place, but Dex had mentioned it was right behind his property, and his place she could find.

She rose and scanned the wardrobe for what to wear. Suddenly, none of her outfits seemed good enough. She picked a blouse, dropped it on the bed, grabbed another, and did the same.

*Wait!* What was she doing? Was she really trying to dress up for Rex?

Tara slapped her cheeks. *Get a grip, girl.*

She finally selected a cream blouse and a pair of jeans, ran a brush through her hair, put on some lip gloss, and left the house.

Tara followed the driveway until she reached the side road. Then she walked down it and spotted Dex's house with the dark blue door. The side road continued past it, and after a few minutes, she reached what she assumed was Rex's place. It seemed similar in structure to Dex's home, except for the large garage attached to it. Since she'd heard the houses had been built to accommodate each brother's interests, Tara assumed that either Rex loved cars or the garage was a workshop of some sort. It reminded her of a certain boy she'd known a long time ago who loved cars as much as he did horses.

She forced the door shut on that memory. Tara hadn't thought of him for ages, and she didn't plan to now. The heartache was best left in the past.

Tara approached the door and knocked. There was no answer, but the door opened slightly instead, and she heard faint strains of what sounded like salsa music.

What was Rex up to? Her curiosity piqued, Tara pushed the door open and stepped in. She glanced around the living room and then stopped short when her eyes reached the kitchen.

Rex was swaying in tune with the music, while making coffee.

Shirtless.

Tara's cheeks warmed. She'd seen lots of chests from her work as a radiologist and had heard guys brag about their washboard abs, but they hadn't seen Rex's. It was perfection, a work of art, especially with the way the muscles rippled and dipped in sync with Rex's moves. If this was what he got from working hard on the ranch, Tara was for it ten thousand percent.

*Get a hold of yourself,* she thought. But she couldn't look away.

Then Rex swiveled, as if realizing there was another presence in the house. "Oh." He picked up a remote and stopped the music.

"Sorry," Tara said, forcing herself to look up from his chest. "The door was open." She kept her face calm as if it was an everyday occurrence to behold such wonderfully shredded abs.

"Give me one minute," Rex said, and he headed off down the hallway. He soon returned wearing a T-shirt, and Tara suddenly missed the view.

What was wrong with her? Why was she obsessing over how hot this guy was?

"Please sit," Rex said, gesturing to the couch. "Would you like some coffee?"

"Yes, please," Tara replied as she sat down. "Black with three teaspoons of milk and half a teaspoon of sugar."

Rex froze in his tracks, though Tara wasn't sure why. Was it what she'd said? She liked her coffee a certain way, but she was fine with plain black if it was too much of a bother. "I'm good with black too."

"No, it's fine. I'll have it ready for you in a second." Rex resumed walking and headed into the kitchen. A few minutes later, he'd returned with two mugs of coffee in hand. "Here you go," he said, passing a grey mug to her.

"Thanks," Tara said, accepting the cup. "You have a lovely place."

"Thank you," Rex replied as he sat opposite her on a smaller couch. "It was all my family's work."

He said it offhandedly, but his tone betrayed the underlying message: *And none of mine.*

And in that moment, Tara caught a glimpse of the vulnerability behind those words and recognized Rex for who he truly was: a wounded soul.

Just like her.

Most people saw her as the confident, career-driven, sometimes fun-loving doctor, but that was because she had perfected her mask, the façade she wanted them to see.

And it seemed he'd done the same. Now she realized what she'd seen of him all along had been a layer and a shield to hide the true him.

What had really happened to Rex? Even though his family had welcomed him with open arms, none of them had asked about the elephant in the room—what made him leave town many years ago. Or maybe they were waiting for him to make the first move. From what Zoey had told her, Rex had behaved in ways completely counter to the actions of the brother Dex had always known, the brother who'd been full of life and loved with everything he had. Tara couldn't imagine that guy from the Rex she'd met, but that didn't mean he wasn't still there hidden behind the mask. What had made him change?

And suddenly, Tara was curious. Maybe it was because of the gentle way he'd handled the horses, or the relaxed way he now spoke to her, but she wanted to know more about him.

The true Rex.

Then she noticed the book on the coffee table.

Her breath hitched. *No, it can't be*.

It'd been so long, but Tara would recognize that book anywhere, considering how many times she'd read it and how dog-eared her copy had ended up. It used to be her second most favorite book after the Bible.

With a trembling hand, she reached out to pick it up, but Rex snatched it up before she could.

She looked up at him. "You're a fan of *Oliver*

*Twist*," she stated, even as her insides twisted into knots.

"Yes," Rex said noncommittally before he lifted his mug to his lips.

Tara said nothing further as she took a sip of her coffee, which, by the way, was delicious. First the garage, and now the book. She'd shut her mind like a steel door against all things Oliver, and yet with just the appearance of the book, the door was already cracking. What were the odds?

Yet even though Oliver had let her down, he'd loved his family very much. He would never have hurt his brother and his family like Rex had done. And Oliver had never been into dancing—he'd said he had two left feet. It was merely a coincidence that Oliver and Rex had the same interests.

"I'm sure you didn't come all this way just to taste my wonderful coffee," Rex said.

*Yes, there it is*. That cocky attitude that was somehow beginning to grow on her. Another reason why Rex couldn't be Oliver—Oliver had been very humble despite being self-assured.

Then he crossed his legs, and Tara's heart rate began to speed up. Strangely, she'd never considered legs an attractive feature in a guy, but Rex was proving her wrong. What was happening to her? Yet she couldn't look away from them.

Rex leaned forward. "Why are you here, Tara?"

"Your legs are hot," she blurted out and almost dropped the mug on the floor.

# CHAPTER 23

Rex grinned even as Tara's face turned bright red. He couldn't believe what he'd just heard. Tara was admiring his legs? He studied the body parts in question. True, they looked great. But she had to be mortified that she'd actually voiced the sentiment.

Yet he liked this Tara—all awkward and embarrassed. She was cute.

"I'm sorry… I didn't mean… Oh, whatever!" She threw up her hands in defeat.

Rex laughed—he couldn't help it.

"This is so awful," she said, covering her face with her hands.

"It's okay," Rex said with a bemused smile.

"No, it's not."

"Thanks for the honest compliment." He chuckled. "Really, it's fine."

"Yet you're still laughing."

"Well, I just wasn't expecting it. Thanks for making my day."

She removed her hands from her face and squared her shoulders. "Okay, I'll just own it. You do have beautiful legs. Masculine, well-toned, and with excellent muscle structure."

It was Rex's turn for his ears to burn. "Can we change the subject?" he said, placing his mug on the coffee table.

Tara set hers down there as well and settled back with a mischievous smile on her face. "I can go on and on in excruciating detail. I studied anatomy after all."

Rex lifted his hands in surrender. "I give up. You win."

A big smile split her face. "Why thank you, my kind gentleman."

Rex couldn't help returning her smile. *Well played, Tara.* Who would have thought he'd be here enjoying a joke with her?

Then her eyes caught his, and Rex couldn't look away. There was just something about Tara that pulled him in, despite his personal reservations about her character.

The air between them sizzled and then grew heavy with tension.

Rex's pulse raced, and his eyes flitted to her lips, the memory of the accidental kiss flashing before him. The neck of his T-shirt suddenly felt tight, and Rex couldn't help tugging at it.

Tara must have felt something too, because she broke eye contact and immediately became preoccupied with drinking her coffee.

An awkward silence ensued between them. Rex already missed the comfortable banter they'd just shared a few moments ago.

Then Tara looked up. "Miss Prissy called," she said abruptly, as if remembering why she'd come to his house in the first place. "She'd like to meet us at noon today at her bed and breakfast. Does that work for you? Oh, and she said to remind you she's your ma's old friend."

Rex felt himself relax, glad for the change of topic. Trust Miss Prissy to pull the Ma card. He mulled over the question. Weston had just informed him that their offer had been accepted—it was the reason he'd been dancing—so he expected his schedule to be busy from now on.

Rex had managed to overcome his dancing handicap with the help of his workers on the ranch in Texas. He wouldn't call himself a great dancer—he was just proficient enough not to step on any toes. He cringed just remembering how bad he'd been before then.

But his schedule was open for now.

"Sure, that works," Rex said to Tara. "I can pick you up a quarter to that time if you like."

"That would be great."

"How about I get your number? I can text you once I'm outside."

"Sounds good to me," Tara said and placed her mug back on the coffee table. She called out her digits, and Rex added them to his phone, then called her number so she had his.

With that settled, Rex focused back on Tara. Who was she anyway? When she'd mentioned how she liked her coffee, he'd almost had a heart attack. Rose had loved hers the same way. How many people did he know that were precise about their coffee in that exact ratio?

But it wasn't possible. Rose was dead. Still, it made Rex curious to know more about her.

"So where did you grow up, Tara?" he asked.

"New York."

Rex's heart skipped a beat. But lots of people grew up in New York, and they weren't Rose. He had to find out more. "High school, college, and medical school?" he asked casually. He couldn't make it obvious what he was digging for.

"A local county high school, Columbia, and Columbia respectively," she said.

Rex tried not to let his disappointment show. If Rose were alive, she would have finished her high school education at a prestigious school, even if it wasn't the one she'd gone to initially. She'd always had lofty educational goals and had the brains to make it happen. Rose wouldn't have gone to a county high school.

As he thought of what to ask her next, Tara finished her coffee and stood up. "I hope you don't mind, but I have to go. There are a few things I need to take care of before noon comes around," she said. "Thanks for the coffee. I'll just take care of the mug and then leave."

Rex rose to his feet as well. Though she'd remained polite, it felt like a wall had suddenly gone up between them. Was it because of the questions he'd asked? It couldn't be—his questions had been innocuous. Maybe he was just imagining things.

"You don't have to do that," he said. "Take care

of the mug, I mean." He took it from her and placed it on the coffee table.

"Alright. Thanks."

He opened the door for her, and she stepped out. Then Rex walked her down the driveway and the path until they reached Dex's house. Tara was quiet the whole way.

"I'll take it from here," she finally said. "Thanks again for the coffee."

"My pleasure," he said. "See you soon."

Then Rex watched her make her way to the main house before she disappeared from view.

But he couldn't help wondering if there was more to Tara than met the eye.

# CHAPTER 24

Tara let out a sigh of relief as she reached the side entrance to the main house. She'd had to skip out of Rex's place as fast as her legs could carry her.

She glanced back in the direction of his home. What was with the twenty questions? She'd responded truthfully, but Tara didn't like anyone digging into her past, and she'd been afraid he might ask a question she couldn't answer. Thankfully, she'd dodged the bullet by hightailing it out of there. Hopefully he'd only been making small talk, nothing more.

Tara had wondered for a second there if Rex was Oliver with the way he'd quizzed her. Oliver would have been the type to probe and probe and eventually crack through her layers, but Rex couldn't be him. Tara would have known.

And then there was the moment they'd shared when their eyes had connected. Rex's gaze had all but sucked her in. Thankfully, Tara had come to her senses in time. Even if she couldn't help being curious about him, nothing romantic could happen between them.

Yet she had to put all that aside for now. Though she was on vacation, Tara had planned to get caught up on her latest research project, and with the upcoming meeting with Miss Prissy, she had less time to work on it before she had to head out.

But she hoped the meeting with Miss Prissy would go well and be done in good time, leaving her room to finish up any outstanding research work she'd slated for today.

"Welcome to Prissy's Bed and Breakfast," Miss Prissy, a buxom lady with a silver bob, said in a pleasant voice with a hint of western drawl.

"It's nice to meet you, ma'am," Tara said. They were in the foyer, a large airy space that boasted beautiful wide-plank hardwood floors, a high ceiling with exposed wood beams, and a long winding staircase. Tara had come by with Zoey the day before to check out her room but hadn't met the owner then.

"You must be Tara. What a lovely young woman. And Rex Dexin. My goodness, it's been years since I've seen you. You were already a strapping young man then, and now you tower over me!"

"A pleasure to see you, ma'am. You look graceful as ever."

Miss Prissy beamed. "Still the flatterer. You Dexin boys were always good at that. Now sit." She led them to a seating area beside the staircase, which was probably where she received her guests.

"Zoey must have told you both about the singles mixer event we're planning," Miss Prissy continued once they were seated. "When we published the news of Dex and Zoey's engagement in our newsletter, we got a flurry of requests for blind dates. Since we'd like to meet as many requests as possible, we figured staging a singles mixer event might be the best way of achieving that goal, even though we don't have a set date yet. But we plan to have enough time to vet each and every attendee. We can't have a creeper in our midst now, can we?"

"How many people are we talking about?" Tara asked.

"Hmm… about twenty-five young men and seventeen ladies," Miss Prissy said.

"I'm surprised there are more interested men."

"It appears news of our success has reached the nearby ranch communities, and it seems local cowboys are interested in our services. But I'm sure that will balance out eventually. I do think it's a good thing."

"Are you looking for something more like speed-dating, where the women sit at the tables and the men circulate from table to table within a certain time limit?" Rex asked. "Or do you want more of a mix and mingle session, where the men and ladies approach whomever they wish to speak to?"

Miss Prissy cocked her head. "Maybe a bit of both? I want everyone to get a chance to talk to someone, and then a section of the program where they get to just mingle as they like."

"Since you already have a good idea of what you want for the event, why do you need us? Anyone can set it up the way you'd like once you give them clear instructions."

"That's a great question, Rex," Miss Prissy said. She leaned forward. "I need you both to be the face of the event."

Tara exchanged glances with Rex. "What do you mean?"

"I'd like the two of you to be the models for any marketing materials, and also be the ones to welcome people to the event. That sort of thing."

A model? Tara hated taking pictures. Besides, that wasn't what she'd signed up for. "I don't think—"

"Oh, you'll do just fine, dear," Miss Prissy said in a voice that brooked no argument. "Now, for example, I'd like you guys to do a test run for the event."

"What's that?" Rex asked.

"Something easy and fun."

"Like right now?" Tara asked.

"Yes."

"But there are only two of us."

"Don't you worry, dear. I have it all planned out." Miss Prissy got up. "Let's head over here." She led them to the dining area Zoey had already shown Tara. But instead of the large rustic dining table and chairs, a small candle-lit table stood in its place with the nearby curtains all closed. Only the bookcase lined on one side of the wall remained the same.

Tara couldn't believe what was in front of her. "Is this supposed to be what I think it is?" she asked. A candlelight dinner was meant to be an intimate affair. How did Miss Prissy expect Rex and her to have one when they'd just barely managed to be comfortable around each other?

"A candlelight dinner? Of course," Miss Prissy said. "Pretend it's evening. You guys will have dinner, while my assistant, Connie, takes pictures. Connie? Where are you?"

"I'm here, Miss Prissy," a young lady with her blonde hair wrapped in a bun called out as she approached them from the other side of the staircase with a camera in her hands. Tara guessed she was coming from the kitchen, one of the areas that was off-limits to guests.

"Connie is my niece but also a talented photographer. She'll make sure the pictures are nice."

"But we aren't dressed for it," Tara protested.

"You look fine. We'd rather have you looking relaxed and comfortable. Right, Connie?"

"Yes, Miss Prissy," Connie replied with a smile.

"Now, now, go ahead and have a seat," Miss Prissy said, shooing them in the direction of the table.

But how were they supposed to pull it off?

Tara felt a hand touch her elbow. "It'll be alright," Rex said. "But are you okay with having your face plastered all over town? I'm guessing this won't only go in the newsletters."

She hadn't even thought about that. But since she

didn't live in Dexin, maybe it was okay? "I'm good with it if you are."

"Oh, I don't care about any of that. But don't worry. I'm here. It'll be okay." Rex pulled out a chair for her, then waited for her to sit before proceeding to his.

"So what do we do now?" Tara whispered from across the table.

Rex smiled, looking oh-so sexy in his rolled-up sleeved shirt, jeans, and boots. He'd left his hat in the SUV. "We chat, and we get to know each other." He leaned forward and extended his hand. "Hello, I'm Rex Dexin. Nice to meet you."

Tara held back a grin as she shook his hand. "Nice to meet you too, Rex. I'm Tara Ellis."

The dinner turned out to be as much fun as Miss Prissy had predicted. Rex made it easy for Tara to open up, and then they talked about everything from books and movies to government affairs. Rex was very knowledgeable and yet fun-loving, and he showed her a side of him that Tara had never seen. Their conversation was so interesting Tara forgot that Connie was taking pictures. By the time the dinner ended, Tara wished they never had to leave.

"I can see you had a good time," Miss Prissy said with a bemused smile.

She'd had a *wonderful* time, but Tara wasn't going there with Miss Prissy. There was a reason she was the town's leading gossip, from what Tara had heard from Zoey.

"Thanks for the dinner," Tara said.

"And the wonderful food," Rex chimed in.

"You're welcome, my dears. Connie, did you get all the photos you need?"

"More than enough," Connie confirmed.

"I'm glad we could help with the event," Tara said.

"Great. Alright, my dears, I need to be off," Miss Prissy said.

"We'll be leaving too," Rex said. "Have a good evening, ma'am. You too, Connie." Connie blushed.

Rex led Tara out of the bed-and-breakfast and into the SUV.

And as he drove them home, Tara couldn't help feeling sad that the night had come to an end.

## CHAPTER 25

Rex sprawled on the king-sized bed in his master bedroom and grinned to himself. What a fun day he'd had. Maybe he'd misjudged Tara—she'd been interesting and down-to-earth with a great sense of humor. Rex had been so relaxed as he'd conversed with her that now he found himself wanting to spend more time with Tara. Because what else would he discover about her? Besides, getting to know Tara didn't mean he'd necessarily get entangled with her romantically.

He rubbed his chin. Now how could he get more time with Tara?

Rex had noticed she'd never ridden any of the horses, even though she showed up each morning at the barn. Considering how she'd been afraid of the horses at first, maybe she didn't know how to ride. Rex could offer to teach her.

He pulled out his phone from his pocket and rose on his elbows. He could send her a message and see what she thought.

**Rex: Hello, Tara.**

Now why did he sound like a dork? Yet she replied almost immediately.

**Tara: Hi! What's up?**

**Rex: I had a good time today.**

**Tara: Me too.**

**Rex: Will you be coming to the barn tomorrow morning? I was wondering if you were interested in learning how to ride.**

He didn't want to assume. She might be busy with something else.

**Tara: Yes, I'd love to.** Her message was accompanied by an excited emoji.

**Rex: Great. See you tomorrow. Have a wonderful evening.**

**Tara: You too. Thanks again.**

Rex dropped his phone on the bed, his face stretched out in a wide smile.

Now he couldn't wait for tomorrow morning to get here.

# CHAPTER 26

Tara practically skipped into the barn the next morning dressed in the horse-riding outfit she'd prepared in advance back when she'd first had the thought of asking Rex to teach her how to ride—shirt, jeans, riding boots, and a helmet on her head. She'd also brought extra treats for the horses, especially Bella, who she'd come to know as the house favorite. Rex was already there and seemed to have already attended to most of the horses.

"Good morning," he said with a smile.

"Good morning," Tara replied. "Did you sleep well?"

"Yes, I did. You sound chipper this morning."

Tara couldn't help bouncing on her toes. "I'm excited about the horse ride."

"If I'd known you'd be this way, I would have offered to teach you much earlier."

"We weren't friends then."

"We are now?"

Tara stilled and cocked her head. "Aren't we?"

"We are," Rex conceded.

She grinned. Of course they'd become friends, if yesterday's meal at Prissy's was anything to go by.

Rex and Tara spent the next hour finishing up the work in the barn. Then Rex saddled one of the docile mares and led her out. "She'll do," he said. "We don't want a horse that'll throw you off its back."

They exited the barn and entered the nearby fenced area. Rex led them to a mounting block he must have placed there earlier.

"I don't need a mounting block," Tara said.

Rex gave her a skeptical look. "Are you sure? It would make it easier for you to learn how to ride."

"I'm good."

"Okay, if you say so," he said, though it was obvious he didn't believe her.

Tara wasn't used to a live horse, but she'd mounted mechanical horses at the amusement park plenty of times. She'd worked there during the summer after she'd finished high school and had taken the ride regularly at the end of her workday to relax. Tara had never thought the experience would come in handy.

Rex led the horse away from the block and selected another spot. "This area should be fine," he said. "First of all, you need to stay alert when you're working with a horse. Don't forget they're huge living beings. So you need to keep an eye on the horse as well as on your surroundings, even including the weather."

"Stay alert," Tara said. "Got it."

"Secondly, you need to make sure the saddle is fitted nice and snug like this," Rex demonstrated, "otherwise it might roll and slip while you're trying to mount. I'll teach you how to saddle the horse next time."

"Okay."

"To mount, you need to do so on the left side of the horse."

"Why?"

"That's the side horses are used to people working with them from. They might get spooked if you try to mount from the right side."

"Left side only. Noted."

"When you mount the horse, hold the reins firmly but not too tight—you want to apply enough pressure so the horse knows to stand still, but not so much that she tries to move away from the pressure. Then place your right hand on the cantle—this raised part of the saddle—and your left hand on her neck." Rex showed her what he meant. "You see that?"

"Got it."

"Place your left foot in the stirrup, making sure the ball of your foot is resting in it like this," he continued. "Then pull yourself up, putting your weight on your left foot and swing your right leg over the horse and to the other side of the saddle, making sure you don't accidentally hit her with that right leg —you don't want to startle her." Rex mounted the horse slowly. "Gently seat yourself in the saddle like this and then place your right leg in its stirrup. We can adjust the length of the stirrup at that point if it doesn't work for you. Does that make sense?"

"Absolutely."

Rex gave her a skeptical look. "It's not too late for us to use the mounting block."

"I'll be fine."

Rex dismounted. "Okay. Why don't you try? I'll hold the horse for you."

Tara followed Rex's instructions and was soon seated in the saddle. She was much higher off the ground than she'd expected.

"Nice."

Tara smirked. "I told you I could do it."

"I don't believe we need to adjust the stirrups in this case. What do you think?"

"Looks and feels good to me."

"Awesome. Now let's make sure you're seated properly. Assume there's an imaginary line running from your shoulders down to your hips and then to your heels. You should be looking forward through the horse's ears. Your arms should be relaxed but close to your body."

"Looking forward, arms relaxed…" Tara made the adjustments.

"Your hands should be roughly level with the saddle, and your shoulders should be up and back , and your back should be straight. You want that imaginary line running from your shoulders to your hips." Tara obeyed. "Your knees and thighs should be able to grip the saddle, and your toes should be pointing upward with your heel downward."

"That's a lot of adjustments."

"It usually feels this way the first time, but eventually, it'll become second nature to you."

"Okay. I think I have that down."

Rex studied her posture. "It looks fair."

"Hey! I'm sure it's better than fair."

"Okay, it looks good for a first timer."

"You just had to qualify it. Give your lady a compliment."

Rex raised his eyebrows. "My lady?"

Tara's ears warmed. "I didn't mean it like that."

"Your posture is excellent, my lady."

"Oh bug off!"

Rex laughed. "Are you sure you want me to do that? Remember, I'm holding the horse for you."

"No," she muttered. It was just like Rex to never let her have the last word.

He laughed again. "Now to come down, do the reverse. Can you try that?"

"Sure." Tara managed to get down without hurting herself.

"Good job. Now let's try this four more times."

Tara obeyed, and each time it got easier. But she hadn't expected her thigh muscles to ache so much.

"How do you feel?" he asked.

"Like a sledgehammer hit my thighs."

"Do you wanna take a break, or do you think you can go on?"

"Let's go on."

"Are you sure?"

"Positive."

"How about I teach you how to stop a horse?"

"Okay."

"I'll demonstrate."

Rex mounted the horse with such fluidity, Tara's mouth fell open. "Wow! That's so cool." Rex looked hot doing it too, but of course she couldn't tell him that.

"Thanks." He grinned with pride. "I've been riding a long time. Now let's get back to the lesson. To get a horse to stop, you need to make sure to slow down before coming to a stop. Don't slam the brakes, so to speak."

"That analogy makes sense. You're good at this teaching thing."

"I've had experience."

"You don't need to puff out your chest."

Rex chuckled. "Now, Miss Tara, can you concentrate? This is important."

"Important. Got it."

"To slow down, sink all your weight into the saddle by leaning back and tensing up your legs. Do you see what I did there?"

"Yes." Those fine legs again. Tara sure wasn't thinking about the horse in that moment.

"Then say 'whoa' in your normal voice and gently pull back the reins. If you tug too hard, you might hurt the horse. If you feel unbalanced, hold the front of the saddle like this to steady yourself."

"Okay."

"Once you've gotten the horse to stop, release your grip on the reins and then pat the horse on the neck as a reward for a job well done. Now I'm going to show you again."

Tara watched as Rex went through the motions. He looked calm and fully in control. "Nice."

"I'll redo it one more time, and then I'll let you have a go at it." Rex repeated the exercise. Then he got off the horse. "Now why don't you give it a try? Don't worry, I'll still hold the horse for you."

"I'm not worried," Tara said, though she totally was. But a lady had to show her bravado. She mounted the mare.

"I'm going to move her slowly now," Rex said. "You might feel awkward and unbalanced at first, but that's natural until you get used to it." He began to walk the horse.

The movement threw Tara off initially, but then she adjusted.

"Now, I need you to stop the horse," Rex directed. "Remember what I said. Slow down not slam the brakes."

Tara did as he instructed and was able to bring the horse to a stop.

"Good job!" Rex said. "We'll try that four more

times." They repeated the exercise a few times. "Now you can dismount." Tara couldn't get down fast enough.

"You did great," Rex praised.

"Thank you."

He rubbed the horse's neck. "You did wonderful," he said to the mare. "Good girl." He retrieved a treat from his pocket and offered it to the mare, who chomped it down eagerly. Then he turned back to Tara. "I think that's enough for today. Make sure you massage those thigh muscles so you don't get too sore tomorrow."

"I will."

"It's time for breakfast, lovebirds!" Becca called out from the front door of the main house.

Tara froze at the words. Lovebirds? Where did that come from? Was Becca up to something? Tara hoped not.

Yet she had a feeling today's breakfast would be interesting.

# CHAPTER 27

"I see you haven't lost your touch," Rex teased Dex as he scooped another spoonful of perfect buttery scrambled eggs into his mouth. Only Tara, Becca, Dex, and Rex were at the breakfast table. Max was already at the ER center, and Jax had gone on yet another business trip. Chloe hadn't woken up yet.

"Why don't you just admit you love my food?" Dex said.

Rex could give him that. "This is delicious," he said, unable to resist taking another spoonful.

"Thanks."

"I see you and Tara are getting along better these days," Becca said.

So that was why she'd made the lovebirds

remark. Rex had pretended not to hear. But he'd noticed Tara had blushed.

"I heard they had a fantastic photoshoot yesterday," Dex said before taking a bite of his toast.

"Really?" Becca's eyes shone with curiosity. "Tell me more."

"There was a candlelight dinner, and they were staring into each other's eyes and laughing and—"

Rex dropped his spoon on the plate. "Where did you hear all this?" What had happened between Tara and him was supposed to be private. And he could see the discussion was making her uncomfortable.

Dex looked at Rex like he'd asked a ridiculous question. "From Miss Prissy of course."

So directly from the horse's mouth. Awesome.

"But you shouldn't let that bug you," Becca said. "It's not like she lied."

Dex snickered, and Rex glared at him. He'd forgotten how hard it was to keep secrets in this family.

"So, have you called Maggie?" Dex asked between bites of food, as if sensing Rex's need to change the topic.

"I'd planned to do so yesterday. Then I realized I didn't have her number." Having a cellphone hadn't been all the rage when he'd left town years ago.

"Why don't you call her now?" Becca said. She retrieved her phone and dialed Maggie's number, placing it in speakerphone mode.

"Becca, how are you?" Maggie answered from the other end of the line.

It felt nice to hear her Bostonian accented voice again. Rex had missed it.

"I'm good," Becca said. "How's the honeymoon?"

"Fantastic, but I'm beginning to miss home. All this traveling is getting to me, but I love the time I'm spending with Peter. How's everyone?"

"We're doing great," Dex said.

"Dex! I didn't know you were there."

"Sorry, I forgot to mention I'd put you on speakerphone," Becca said.

"No worries. How's my grandbaby?"

"She's still sleeping."

"Give her a kiss for me when she wakes up, will you?"

"Will do."

"Maggie, there's someone here that wants to speak with you," Dex said.

"Who?"

"Hello, Maggie," Rex said.

There was an audible gasp from the other end of

the line. "No, it can't be…"

"Yes, it's me."

"Oh my goodness," Maggie began to cry.

Rex grew uncomfortable. He'd never heard Maggie sob, and now he was the cause of it.

"Maggie, stop crying. It's okay," Becca said.

"Rex, you're back. You're finally back," Maggie said between sobs. Then she sniffled. "No. This isn't the time to cry. Peter! You need to start packing. We're going home!"

"You don't have to do that," Rex protested.

"My baby is back, and I'm coming home," Maggie stated firmly. "I'll see you all in a few days. I have to go pack. Bye!" The call disconnected.

Rex leaned back. Maggie was coming home. "She didn't have to."

"She's been praying for you to come home every night for as long as I remember," Dex said quietly. "I can't imagine how excited she was to hear your voice."

Maggie had been like his second Ma, and Rex had missed her.

But it also meant the time to open up about Tammy was near.

Because Rex knew that even if no one else asked, Maggie would.

# CHAPTER 28

Tara followed Rex out of the main house after breakfast was done and all the dishes had been washed and left to dry. She'd seen a pensive look on his face after the call and sensed something was weighing heavy on his mind. "Rex, are you okay?" She could ask, since they were friends now, right?

"I'll be fine." He headed down the driveway.

Tara went after him. "Do you want to talk about it?"

He halted and studied her. "Would you like to take a walk?"

"Sure." She needed it after the heavy breakfast she'd just had.

Rex led her down a path she'd never noticed

before. Soon they reached a giant oak tree that wasn't very far from a nearby lake. Rex stood on the bank, picked some smooth stones, and began to toss them into the lake. Tara stayed silent by his side. He'd speak whenever he was ready.

"It's time I told them about Tammy," he finally said.

"Who's Tammy?" Tara asked.

"The lady I left town with. Max's ex-girlfriend."

Tara hadn't known her name was Tammy, though she'd heard about her.

"She loved Max with everything in her heart," Rex continued. "They'd planned their wedding, and she'd been all excited about becoming his wife. Most folks thought I had a crush on her, but that wasn't true. She was like the big sister I never had." He tossed another stone into the water. "A few days before the wedding, she started having mild abdominal pains. She thought it was just something she'd eaten, but I urged her to go to the hospital, where they ran a bunch of tests. Tammy didn't want Max to worry, so she didn't tell him. The day before the wedding, she got the test results back: she had pancreatic cancer and only had a few months to live."

Tara's breath caught. That must have been devastating.

"I found her crying by this oak tree," Rex said. "She couldn't imagine putting Max through a wedding only to have her death crush him. So she was planning to disappear. Alone. I wouldn't have known if I hadn't found her here. No matter how much I pleaded with her to tell Max, her mind was made up.

"But I couldn't let her go alone. I knew what it meant to lose someone without being able to help, and I couldn't let that happen again. Tammy had no family—Max was everything to her. And I didn't think Max would want her to be on her own. So I withdrew my inheritance and left with her. Leaving with no word to Max kept bothering me, so at the train station, I met one of my classmates named Oscar and snuck him a note to give to Max. He promised to deliver it, but now I've realized that never happened."

That Oscar fellow didn't sound like a good guy.

Rex threw another stone in the lake and watched as the water rippled. "We eventually reached Texas and got a place close to a renowned cancer institute. I'd heard about the hospital, and I wanted us to give it a shot. I felt that if she could survive the cancer, then we could always come back home to Max. For a while she got better, and we thought she'd beaten it.

I'd bought a house with space for some animals, and Tammy loved spending time with them. They made the regular check-ups easier to handle. But then the cancer came roaring back, and I lost her soon after.

"I couldn't handle the loss. For weeks, I was in a daze. I wanted to bring her body back home, but we'd spent most of my inheritance on her treatments, and it had run out. So I started bronc riding both to drown my thoughts of her and make some money. It was during one of those events that I met Weston and Liam, and we decided to start a horse business together, which eventually grew to be successful. But every time I thought about coming home, I remembered how heartbroken Max would be, and I couldn't do it. So the years passed by until my partners needed to return to the east coast, and I figured it was as good a time as any to face my demons."

So it hadn't been Rex's fault, just like Dex had said. Rex had given up his family and his dreams to save another, who wasn't even his sweetheart.

Rex looked so forlorn standing there that Tara couldn't stop herself from reaching out and wrapping her arms around him.

She felt his shoulders shudder, and then he leaned into her.

Tara just held him, comforting the boy inside

who'd lost once and then again. After a few minutes, when she was sure he'd calmed down, Tara released him.

"Thank you so much," he said.

Tara had experienced loss before, so she knew how all the regrets and helplessness could hurt and consume you if you let them. She gave him a warm smile. "Glad these shoulders could help," she said.

Rex smiled and tapped the tip of her nose.

"What was that for?"

"For being your sassy self. Thank you."

Tara shrugged, though she appreciated his words. "That's what friends are for. Who would have thought that I'd become friends with Mr. Obnoxious?"

Rex lifted an eyebrow. "That's what you called me?"

"Sure. You were quite a pain in the neck."

"Look who's talking. I thought you had a split personality."

Tara punched his shoulder. "Hey! That's not fair."

"But I know better now. You were probably just having a bad day."

"To be honest, I cringe whenever I think about my behavior that day. It was uncalled for."

"Your apology is accepted."

"Thank you."

"So what are your plans for today?" Rex asked.

"Nothing much. Just lounging around since I'm on vacation. I'll probably spend some time with Zoey, but that's it. I've been so busy with work that all I want to do is relax. What about you?"

"My partners and I just bought a piece of property here in Dexin."

"Wow! Congratulations."

"Thanks. You're the first person I've told."

Tara put her hand on her chest. "I feel honored. What's the place like?"

Rex's face held a faraway look. "It's a beauty. Lots of hills and meadows. There's still a lot of work to do on it and some extra permits to get before it'll be ready. But we'll get it done."

"That sounds exciting. So you're back in Dexin for good."

He nodded. "I feel it's the right decision. But what about you? How are you finding Dexin? It's a different pace of life than New York."

"It's nice. But I've been here before, many, many years ago."

"Really? When?"

Could she tell him? She'd never told anyone about Oliver.

Her phone rang.

Tara pulled it out from her pocket and scanned the screen. "It's Miss Prissy." She swiped the answer button. "Hello, Miss Prissy."

"Hello, dear. How are you doing today?"

"Fine, ma'am."

"I just wanted to let you know the pictures are out, and they look marvelous. I'm going to send you a few examples so you see what I mean."

"Thank you."

"And don't be afraid to chase him if you like him."

What was she talking about? "Excuse me?" Wait, did she mean Rex? Tara looked at him.

"The photos say it all," Miss Prissy said. "It's obvious you adore each other."

That was not possible. Miss Prissy must be reading meaning into things. Tara and Rex had only just become friends.

"I have to go," Miss Prissy continued. "We've got so much planning to do for the event. Talk to you later, honey." The line went dead.

"What did she say?" Rex asked.

"The photos are out." There was no way Tara was telling him everything Miss Prissy had said.

Her phone pinged with an alert, and she saw a message had come in.

Tara opened it, and her heart sank as she stared at the pictures Miss Prissy had sent her.

She really was done for.

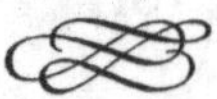

# CHAPTER 29

"Are you okay?" Rex asked. "You look like you've seen a ghost."

"I'm fine," Tara said, though he could tell she wasn't. "It's just something I need to take care of."

"Okay." She seemed distracted. "Maybe we should head back."

"That would be great."

This time it was Tara that stayed silent all the way back, even until they arrived in front of the main house.

"Are you sure everything is alright?" Rex asked. Was it something Miss Prissy had said to her?

Tara flashed him a small smile. "I just have some things to think about. But I'll be okay. I promise."

"Let me know if you ever want to talk."

"I will. Thanks for trusting me earlier. I won't mention our discussion to anyone."

"I should be the one thanking you for listening." He appreciated how she'd supported him when he'd had heavy things on his mind.

And now he wanted more.

"Would you like to come over to my place for dinner?" he blurted out. "I make a mean spaghetti and meatballs, and Becca could use the time off. I'm sure Dex and Zoey can arrange their own meal if I let them know." Now he was rambling.

"Sure." Tara seemed surprised but pleased. "I think Zoey and Dex already have a date, and I don't believe Jax will be back today."

Rex was happy she'd accepted. "I look forward to seeing you tonight then."

"Okay. Bye." She waved at him and then entered the house.

Rex headed home with a spring in his step. But was this supposed to be a date? He didn't know, but there was no need to analyze it, and it might not necessarily be anything more.

All he had to do was enjoy their time together as friends, right?

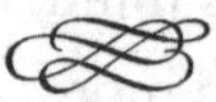

# CHAPTER 30

Tara collapsed on her bed. Then she rolled to her side. Her mind couldn't stop thinking about the pictures.

Fortunately, Rex hadn't seen them. She pulled up one again and stared at it, noting the twinkle in her eyes and the way she'd looked at him. Anyone could see she was enamored with Rex. Tara tossed the phone on the bed and covered her face with her hands.

How had it happened? She'd successfully guarded her heart for so long, yet just an encounter with this cowboy already had her walls crashing down.

She let out a huge sigh. This was the worst thing

that could have happened to her when she had no hope of ever having a family.

Yet, she couldn't deny that her heart wanted to grow even closer to him. She'd been pleased that he'd trusted her enough to open up to her, and it had made her ache for the camaraderie that came from being vulnerable with the one you cared about.

Tara ran her hands through her hair. *What am I going to do?*

She needed to shut this down before it went any further. Before Rex got hurt when he discovered who she was and what she'd done.

But didn't Tara deserve to experience a little happiness in her life?

Maybe she could just enjoy this one evening with him before letting everything go.

# CHAPTER 31

Rex opened his door to see Tara standing in front of him, looking as lovely as ever in a purple dress shirt paired with cowboy boots, the combination offsetting the colors of her eyes. "You look beautiful," he said.

Tara blushed. "Thank you. You don't look so bad yourself." Rex had worn a grey dress shirt with rolled up sleeves. "Here's a bottle of non-alcoholic wine."

Rex accepted the bottle, and his eyebrows rose at the choice. "It's my favorite. How did you know?"

She seemed pleased at his words. "A little birdie might have mentioned it."

If he had to guess who the birdie was, Rex would put his money on Dex, since they'd both shared a bottle or two in the past. "Thank you," he said. "Please come in." He made the way for her to enter, and then he shut the door behind him. "This way."

Rex led her down the hallway until they reached the sunroom, and then he flung the French doors open. The idea had come to him earlier this afternoon, and he'd thought Tara might appreciate it.

"Oh, wow!" Tara said. "This is beautiful."

"Thank you. I'm glad you like it." Rex had wanted to create a rustic version of the candlelight dinner but with a cowboy flair to it. He'd replaced the white table linen and napkins with blue-checkered ones and hung candle lanterns all over the sunroom instead of having candles on the table, all without obstructing the view of the sky through the glass.

He helped her get seated and then approached the serving table he'd placed on the side. "For appetizers we have cowboy caviar—a simple mix of corn, black beans, black-eyed peas, tomatoes, peppers, onion, and avocado with a drizzle of balsamic vinaigrette dressing, and then we have bite-sized caprese salad—fresh mozzarella and cherry tomatoes on basil-leaf-covered snack crackers. Which would you like?"

"I'll have the caprese salad, thank you." She tried to rise, but Rex stopped her.

"Please sit," he said. "I'll serve you tonight." A look of surprise and then pleasure crossed her face.

Rex brought the caprese salad to her and took the cowboy caviar for himself before sitting down. "Would you like to say a prayer?" he asked.

Tara smiled and obliged him, and then they began to eat. She took a bite of the salad and moaned in pleasure.

The sound went straight to his core. How was he going to survive this dinner if she continued like this?

"This is so good," she said. "I didn't know you could cook."

The corners of his lips turned up at her words. "I'm not as good as Dex, but I have a few tricks in my bag. What about you? Do you cook?"

"Sometimes. I can if I have to, but I like to keep it simple."

"Me too," Rex said. "I'd rather leave all the elaborate cooking to Dex."

"I do the same too. But I really like yours. You can't beat good simple cooking."

Rex chuckled. "Thanks for the ego boost."

They soon finished the appetizers, and Rex cleared the dishes.

"Next up, we have the main course," he said. "The options are spaghetti and meatballs or spaghetti and meatballs." Tara laughed. "Hey, I wanted to make something I was sure I was good at!"

"I'll take spaghetti and meatballs then," she said with an amused smile.

"Coming right up." He served the dishes, and they dug in. Rex watched as Tara took a forkful.

"Oh wow!" she said.

"You like?"

"I love it! You do make a mean spaghetti and meatballs."

Rex leaned back, satisfied with her praise. He was glad the date—no, dinner—was going great. They chatted and laughed as they ate, and by the time they were done, Rex was more in *like* with her than when dinner had started. He removed their empty plates.

"Now we have dessert," he said. "Chocolate fudge ice cream and coffee ice cream."

Tara's eyes narrowed. "How did you know I liked chocolate fudge ice cream?"

Rex shrugged. "I cheated and asked Zoey."

Tara fought to hide her smile. "You cheated alright, but I forgive you because I really do love chocolate fudge ice cream with a scoop of coffee ice cream on the side."

"Coming right up." Rex served scoops of ice

cream into two small crystalline bowls and handed one to her.

"You like chocolate fudge ice cream too?"

Rex shook his head. "Coffee ice cream is my favorite, but I want to see why you love yours."

Tara watched him take a spoonful. "So what do you think?"

"It's actually nice. I still prefer a solo coffee ice cream, but this is a close second."

"Yes! One more convert."

Rex raised an eyebrow. "You have others?"

"Yep! Zoey is one. I almost got Dex on it, but he quickly jumped off the train."

Rex laughed. "You're funny, you know that, right?"

"So I've been told." Tara took a spoonful of her ice cream and then another. Then she noticed he was staring at her. "What?"

"There's a little ice cream at the corner of your mouth."

"Here?" She touched her napkin at the right side of her mouth.

"No. The other side."

"What about now?" She'd dabbed at the left side of her mouth.

"Close. Hold on, let me help." Rex leaned

forward and used his thumb to remove the little glob of ice cream, then dabbed his finger clean on his napkin. "There. All gone." Then he realized Tara was staring at him.

The air between them crackled.

Rex could see the pulse ticking at the base of her throat, and his eyes went to her lips. They looked soft and inviting, and he wanted to taste them. But would she pull back?

He inched his face closer to hers, waiting to see what she would do, but Tara didn't move away.

His eyes met hers. Rex felt the pull tighten between them. Still, Tara's eyes stayed locked onto his, and she leaned in instead.

She was so beautiful and warm and honest. How could Rex resist the invitation?

His hand grazed the side of her cheek, leaving feathery touches in its wake.

Her breath hitched. And in that moment, he didn't think he could hold himself back much longer.

So he drew closer and kissed her.

Tara's lips were soft as he'd imagined, delicate, like a flower to be treasured. The scent of summer and warm beaches and coconuts with a hint of vanilla wrapped around him until it was all he could breathe in, sending his insides into overdrive.

Rex deepened the kiss. It was like everything else faded away, leaving only the two of them in a place full of sweetness, tenderness, and warmth, and Rex wished it would never end.

But he had to hold back for her sake.

So Rex released her.

# CHAPTER 32

*Wow! Wow! Wow!* Those words were all that ran through Tara's mind as she leaned back and absorbed what had just happened. Rex's kisses were the best dessert ever. She'd never thought it was possible, but chocolate fudge ice cream didn't even come close. Tara wished for more, but she couldn't really be Oliver Twist now, could she?

Rex settled back into his seat and continued eating his dessert like nothing had happened. But now Tara couldn't take her eyes away from those lips—she wanted to devour them once more. But she couldn't be forward about it, which meant this had been her one-time experience with them before she had to let go.

The thought soured her mood. How could she go back to regular everyday life after this? The whole evening had been wonderful, and the thought of not spending more time with Rex depressed her. Kisses aside, she enjoyed being with him. But what choice did she have? It was better to let him down now than later, when he'd be hurt more.

"You don't like your dessert anymore?" Rex asked with a look of concern on his face.

"Oh, I do." She'd forgotten about the dessert that was actually in her bowl. "I love them both."

Rex must have caught her meaning because his face went all red. But then he leaned forward. "I'm glad you enjoyed them," he said in a low voice. "Would you like more?"

It was Tara's turn to blush. *Oh my goodness gracious*. Did he mean the ice cream or the kiss?

Rex chuckled when she didn't answer and went back to eating his dessert.

Tara finished the ice cream in her bowl and then leaned back, totally satiated. "Thanks for the meal. This was delightful."

Rex set down his spoon. "I'm glad you loved it."

She'd had a great time, but the sky had darkened, and it was getting late. "Unfortunately, it's time for me to leave," she said as she rose to her feet. But I'll do so after cleaning up the dishes."

Rex stood up. "Please, you don't have to. I'll take care of them."

"It's not a problem. It's my way of saying thank you for a wonderful dinner. Or we could do them together."

But Rex wouldn't back down. "I insist," he said. "It's not a big deal. I'll walk you home instead."

This man could be stubborn when he wanted to be. And honestly, Tara didn't mind *not* doing the dishes. "Okay. Thanks."

She left the house with Rex by her side. The walk was much shorter than Tara would have liked, and soon they were back at the main house.

But Rex pulled her into a shadowed area.

"What's wrong?" Tara asked, her heart beating loudly against her chest. She had an idea of what he wanted, and she hoped it would come true.

"Just more dessert," Rex said. And then he kissed her again.

Tara would have thought it impossible, but this kiss was even better than the last one. Rex tasted sweet like chocolate yet heady like coffee, and sparks of electricity shot through her skin as his hands wove into her hair and cupped the back of her head.

The butterflies in her belly went crazy. Tara looped her arms around his neck, deepening the kiss, and indulging in the unapologetic, masculine scent that was all Rex. The kiss was heady, intoxicating, and Tara couldn't get enough.

Rex eventually broke the kiss and rested his forehead against hers, holding her in his arms like a treasure he'd found and couldn't let go.

"Tara, would you go out with me?" he asked.

She froze. This was the opposite of what she had to do. Accepting Rex would mean hurting him in the end, since she'd never be able to marry him or have a family.

It was better to let him go now, it was everything her head was telling her, but her heart hurt just thinking of turning him down. Didn't she deserve a little bit of happiness, however brief it might turn out to be? A chance to have memories she could look back to, instead of regrets from never trying? And how could she even say no, after what they'd just shared? Especially since she didn't want to *say* no.

So Tara went against everything her mind screamed at her.

"Yes, I'll go out with you," she said.

# CHAPTER 33

ex couldn't believe it. Tara had said yes. He hadn't planned to ask her out, but it had felt right in that moment, and he'd taken the chance.

He'd never thought it possible, but Tara had touched a part hidden within him Rex had thought dead—he'd not been interested in any other lady since Rose.

And Rex really liked her. Of course they had their differences, especially with him being a country boy and her a city girl, but who said love couldn't cross boundaries? It was like she got him on a deeper level. Besides, they could tackle their differences one by one.

For now, he had to let her go. "Thanks for saying

yes," he said, touching her cheek and then tucking her hair behind her ear. "I'll see you tomorrow. Have a wonderful night, okay?"

Tara nodded. "You too."

He gave her one last tender kiss before releasing her.

Rex watched her walk away and then turn to wave at him before entering the house. He waved back.

Then he headed to his place. Tara was now his girlfriend. Who would have imagined it? But the thought had Rex grinning like a fool.

He'd had a fantastic evening, but Rex was now more excited about what tomorrow would bring.

# CHAPTER 34

Tara shut the main door behind her and turned to make her way up the stairs.

"That was hot!" a familiar voice said.

Tara jumped on seeing Zoey standing in front of her. "What are you doing here?" And how had she even seen them?

"I came to drop off a case of strawberries for Becca, since she was craving them, but I didn't expect to see Rex devouring my soul sister. You've been busy, my friend."

"You're crazy," Tara said. She walked past Zoey and headed up the stairs, but Zoey followed at her heels. "Like you and Dex are not up to it too."

Tara entered her room and sat on the damask-covered king-sized bed.

Zoey followed her in and flopped down beside her. "But do you like him? I thought you guys didn't get along."

Tara turned and faced her friend. "I do like him. I didn't think I would, but I do."

"Does he like you too?"

"Well, he asked me out."

Zoey's eyes widened, and she grabbed Tara's shoulders. "And? What did you say?"

"I said yes."

Zoey wrapped her into a hug. "I'm so happy for you. It's been a long time coming."

Tara hugged her back. "Thank you. But you can't tell anyone."

Zoey released her. "Why not? Does he want you to keep it a secret?"

"No, nothing like that. I know he's trying to readjust to being back with the family, and he could do without any extra pressure from his brothers. I'd like him to reveal it at his own pace."

Zoey gave her an incredulous look. "Wow! Are you still my friend Tara?"

"I still am. Let's just say I'm a bit protective of him."

Zoey's eyes searched Tara's face. "You love him," she stated.

Love? Tara wasn't sure, but she found she didn't loathe the idea. "I don't know about that, but I just want him to be happy. He's one of the good guys."

Zoey chuckled. "Sorry, my friend, but you've been bitten by the love bug. But I won't tell Dex. I'm just happy you're happy." She gave Tara another hug. "Yay! My best friend is in a relationship! Finally! Okay, I'll go for now. I'm sure you want to spend some time thinking about that kiss." She winked at Tara.

"You're crazy!" Tara threw a pillow at Zoey's head.

Zoey laughed as she evaded it. "Goodnight, my lovesick friend," she said cheerily. She blew Tara a kiss and then left.

Tara relaxed on the bed, and a big smile split her face. Zoey was right. She did want to think about the kiss—kisses, actually. They'd been the best ever.

But more than that, she looked forward to what a relationship with Rex would be like.

# CHAPTER 35

"Oh my goodness, I can't believe it's you, after all these years," Maggie said as she cradled Rex's face in her hands. Then she smacked his shoulder. "You naughty boy, why didn't you come back earlier?"

Rex rubbed his shoulder. He didn't remember Maggie being this strong. But she looked amazing in a blouse and a pair of slacks. "I'm sorry."

She gave him a pointed look. "Now make sure you don't disappear again."

Maggie didn't have to worry about that. "Yes, ma'am." Then he pulled her into a hug. She smelled of cinnamon and vanilla. Of home. "I've missed you."

"Of course you have." She patted his back. "Now

release me and let me introduce you to the love of my life." Rex let her go and then straightened. "Rex, meet Peter Taylor, my husband extraordinaire."

The dashing middle-aged man with intelligent blue eyes in a sports coat, shirt, and jeans laughed and extended a hand to Rex. "Nice to meet you, Rex. I've heard so much about you."

"It's an honor to meet you, sir," Rex said as he shook Peter's hand. The handshake was firm and confident, just like he'd expected. "Sorry I didn't get to meet you before the wedding."

Peter chuckled. "Oh, I'm glad about that. Dex and Jax gave me a hard enough time as it was."

"And this must be Tara," Maggie said, reaching for her and pulling her into a hug.

Tara returned the hug. "It's nice to finally meet you, Maggie," she said. "Welcome home."

"Oh my, you're such an old soul," Maggie said. "You have to let the burdens go, okay?" She patted Tara's back and then released her.

Rex glanced at Tara. Had something been weighing her down? Of course, he was curious as to what that might be, but he resolved to wait until whenever Tara felt comfortable enough to share it with him.

"Now, now, let's sit," Maggie said, motioning to

the couches in the living room. "Rex, you sit beside me." She patted the spot by her side. Rex obeyed and everyone found a place. Even Max had managed to make it home on time, and he now sat beside Becca on one of the loveseats. Only Jax was missing.

As Rex thought about it, he realized Jax had been absent from home a lot these days. Rex had given him space at first, but maybe he needed to have a chat with him to find out what was going on.

"So how are you, my dear?" Maggie asked Rex.

"I'm fine," he replied. "Congratulations on your wedding and honeymoon. I hear I just missed seeing you at the Dexington's."

Maggie patted his hand. "I should have known you were coming home when I dreamt about your ma."

Rex shot her a look of surprise. "You did?"

"Mm-hmm. I usually do when something good is about to happen to one of you boys. But I thought it was because Dex got engaged. I also remember you were heavy on my mind about two months ago, but at that time I just kept praying about it. Did anything happen then?"

"I had a major elbow injury."

Maggie's face grew concerned. "Are you okay now?" She grabbed his arm and examined it.

"That's the wrong arm," Rex said. Everyone chuckled. "But I had surgery on it, and it's fine now."

Maggie's face relaxed. "Thank the Lord for that."

Then her eyes searched Rex's face. "How's Tammy?"

The whole room went as silent as a grave.

This was the moment Rex had been dreading. He glanced at Tara, and she gave him a tiny nod.

Rex took a deep breath. He couldn't avoid it any longer. "Tammy passed away from pancreatic cancer."

Soft gasps filled the room. But Tara gave him an encouraging smile.

Rex proceeded to tell his family what had happened. The whole time he kept his eyes fixed on Max and watched for his reaction, but Max stayed still as a statue and said nothing. Becca clutched his hand tightly in hers.

"I'm so sorry, Max," Rex said softly as he finished.

"You should have told me," Max said. "Do you know how it feels to find out I let down the person I loved?"

"I'm sorry, Max," Rex pleaded.

Max shot to his feet. "I should have had a choice! You took that from me. Now all I have left is the regret of not knowing and not being there for her."

"I'm sorry," There was nothing else to say. He'd done this to Max.

"I think I'm going to need a moment," Max said and stalked off.

Becca stood as well. "He just needs a little time. I'll be right back." She hurried after Max.

Rex put his face in his hands. He'd messed up big time. What if Max never forgave him?

Then he felt a hand touch his arm, and he looked up. It was Tara. "It's going to be alright," she whispered.

Rex nodded. He had to believe that—he didn't want to lose his family again.

"Rex, look at me," Maggie said. He obliged. Her eyes shone with unshed tears.

Then she wrapped her arms around him. "I'm sorry you had to bear it all alone."

And that was when Rex broke down and cried. It had been so hard—watching Tammy die little by little before his eyes. Over the next few minutes, it was like all the sorrow and grief that had built up within him collapsed and gushed out, eventually leaving him drained.

Soon Rex felt more arms around him. "I'm sorry we weren't there for you," Dex said.

Then more arms joined—it was like everyone had piled on. Rex didn't know how long they stayed that way, but it felt good to have his family's understanding.

"Now, let the boy breathe," Maggie said and shooed them away. There was laughter, and then Rex felt arms leave him. He looked up to see Max standing in front of him.

Max pulled Rex to his feet. They stood there, brothers facing and staring at each other. Then Max hugged Rex. "I forgive you," he said.

Those words were the balm that Rex's soul had needed for so long, the words he'd waited forever to hear. In that moment, the weight that had chained him down over the years released him.

Tears filled Rex's eyes. "Thank you," he said.

But Max wasn't finished. "I'm sorry I gave up on you when you didn't come home. I should have looked for you."

"It's not your fault," Rex said.

Max shook his head. "No, it is. I knew the kind of man you were, and I shouldn't have let the hurt blind me. Will you forgive me?"

Rex nodded. Max didn't need his forgiveness—

he'd done nothing wrong, but Rex would give it if it made Max feel better.

He pulled back to look Max in the eye. "I brought her home, like she'd always wanted." He'd had her cremated, and her ashes were sealed in the cylindrical bag.

"Then we should have a service for her," Becca suggested. "And bury her on the property."

Max released Rex and glanced at Becca. "You don't mind?"

"No," she said. "I have you now because she first loved you and taught you how to love."

"That sounds like a good plan," Maggie said. "Maybe we should hold it this evening."

The family discussed further and decided to bury her under the oak tree, since it had been Tammy's favorite spot on the property. Maggie made a quick call to the pastor of their family church, and he agreed to preside over the service.

Later that evening, everyone—except for Peter, who was looking after Chloe back at the house— arrived at the oak tree by the lakeside dressed in white instead of black, since it was one of Tammy's favorite colors. Max, Dex, and Rex had selected and dug a spot under the oak tree and nailed a wooden headstone to the tree trunk.

The pastor led them in a hymn and a prayer. Everyone got a chance to say something nice about Tammy. Even Becca thanked her for loving Max, and Tara thanked her for bringing Rex home to his family.

Then Max lowered the cylindrical urn into the ground, and Dex and Rex sealed the grave. There was a final benediction, and the service was over. Most people returned to the main house. Max lingered for a few minutes and then left with Becca, leaving Rex standing at the gravesite.

A hand touched his, and Rex turned to see Tara by his side. He wrapped his arm around her and pulled her close, grateful for her presence.

"How are you feeling?" Tara asked.

"I'm okay," Rex said. "It feels good to have everything out in the open, and to know she's finally home like she wanted. I know she's already in heaven, but it's nice to bring closure to this too."

Tara leaned her head on his shoulder. "I'm glad you're alright."

Rex kissed the top of her head. "Thanks for being with me. I know it's not the ideal way to start a relationship."

"I don't mind."

They stayed quiet for a few more moments,

feeling the warm breeze from the lake and inhaling the fresh, flower-scented air.

"I think it's time to go," Rex said. "Goodbye, Tammy."

Then Rex and Tara turned and headed back the way they'd come.

They arrived at the main house and found Becca lounging on the large couch. "I'm so exhausted," she said.

"As well you should be," Maggie said from where she stood in the kitchen. "Now, no more cooking or household chores for you, sweet girl."

"I should protest, but I accept, Maggie," Becca said. "The guys have been helping so much, but I get tired so easily these days."

"When is your next doctor's appointment?" Zoey asked. She and Dex were helping Maggie in the kitchen, and Tara moved to join them.

Rex touched her arm. "Do you need my help?" he whispered.

"We've got this covered," Tara whispered back and winked at him before going to Zoey's side.

"My appointment is next week," Becca said and

yawned, oblivious to the conversation between Rex and Tara.

"You should head to bed and take a nap," Rex suggested as he leaned against the wall.

"Maybe I will."

"And you can send Chloe out if she's awake. We'll keep her busy for you."

Becca gave Rex a grateful smile. "That would be great."

"Where's Max by the way?"

"He's talking shop with Peter. Some sort of meeting about the hospital." Becca yawned again. "I'll see you guys later." Then she made her way to their section of the house.

A few minutes later, Chloe came running down the hallway and then screeched to a halt. Her eyes searched the living room and spotted Rex.

"Uncle Rex!" she cried out and launched herself at him.

Rex opened his arms and caught her. "How are you?"

She beamed. "I'm fine." Then her face turned serious. "Wait! Let me down."

Rex did as she'd requested, and she took off. "I'm coming!" she shouted back at him as she raced to their wing. Moments later, Chloe returned with some-thing pink in her hand.

"Here. This is for you," she said.

It was a pair of pink socks, like Dex had mentioned before.

Rex accepted the gift. "Thank you, Chloe."

Chloe's face brightened. "You're welcome. You have to show me when you wear them, Uncle Rex."

"Yes, ma'am."

Then she cocked her head. "So, Uncle Rex?"

"What is it, Chloe?"

"Did you kiss Aunt Tara?"

# CHAPTER 36

The sounds from the kitchen ceased even as Rex fought to hide his surprise. How had Chloe known? And now it seemed all ears were curious to hear the answer to her question.

"Well, did you kiss Aunt Tara?" she asked again.

"Now, Chloe, you shouldn't ask your uncle that question," Maggie chided gently.

"Sorry, Grandma," Chloe said with a contrite voice. "But Mummy told Daddy they kissed."

*Great*. More people knew?

"Inquiring minds would like to know the answer to that question," Dex said from the kitchen.

Rex stole a glance at Tara, but she kept her face locked on the dish in front of her. It was up to him to handle it, and he couldn't allow her to be embarrassed in any way.

He stooped before his niece. "Chloe?"

"Yes, Uncle Rex?" Her innocent blue eyes held his.

"Aunt Tara is my girlfriend, so yes, I kissed her." He glanced at Tara's direction and noticed she was smiling at him.

His shoulders relaxed. *Good*. He hadn't messed up.

"I knew it!" Dex said.

"Oh my goodness, that's wonderful!" Maggie said. "When did this happen? Zoey, you don't seem surprised."

Zoey shifted uncomfortably. "I found out last night. Sorry, Dex, I promised I wouldn't tell you."

"No worries, babe, I understand," Dex said. Then he turned to Rex. "Rex, my man." Dex grinned like he'd won the lottery.

"Oh give him a break," Maggie said, smacking Dex's shoulder. "I don't want any of you giving them a hard time."

"Yes, ma'am," Zoey and Dex chorused.

"In fact, you two should get out of here. Shoo! Go do whatever new lovebirds do. Zoey, Dex, and I can handle everything here."

"I can still help," Tara protested.

"Don't you worry, dear," Maggie said. "We have more than enough hands to help. And I'm sure that young man over there would like another opportunity to give you a kiss."

"Maggie!" Rex said. He'd forgotten Maggie could be a tease when she wanted to be.

Tara's face went all red, while Dex and Zoey cracked up.

"Now go if you don't want to hear anything more from us," Maggie said.

Tara came out of the kitchen. "You guys are ganging up on us."

"For good reason," Zoey retorted. "Now go and kiss him well for all of us." She blew a kiss at Tara.

"You're crazy," Tara said.

Zoey laughed. "And I love you too."

Rex watched their exchange. What had he signed up for with these two as friends? But truth be told, it wasn't like his brothers were any better in the teasing department.

"Bye, Chloe," he said, ruffling her hair.

"Bye, Uncle Rex," she said without looking up. She'd found a coloring book and crayons and had already busied herself with them.

Then Rex took Tara's hands and led her out of the house.

He leaned against the wall a few feet away from the main door, and Tara did the same.

"I can't believe these guys," Tara said. "Even Chloe heard about the kiss."

Rex chuckled. "I couldn't believe my ears when she said it."

Tara glanced at him. "Were you embarrassed?"

Rex shook his head. "Not really. But I didn't want to put you in a tough spot."

Tara shrugged. "I'm good. Of course, I would have preferred if the relationship wasn't yet public knowledge, but that was only because I thought you might not want your family to know yet. For privacy reasons."

He appreciated how she thought on his behalf. "True. Yet they would have found out one way or the other—they're a tenacious bunch when it comes to matters of the heart—and I already knew they'd accept you. Now come here." He pulled her into his arms.

"What are you doing?"

Rex gave her a mischievous smile. "I believe they gave us an assignment. Something about a kiss," he said in a lowered voice.

"Oh please, you just want some."

"That I do. I admit it. I do enjoy kissing you."

Her face turned red. "How can you even say that with a straight face?"

"Now may I?"

She held up a finger. "It depends."

"On what?"

"On how well you convince me," she teased.

"Oh dear lady of New York," Rex said in his most British voice, "would you give this young knight a kiss for the evening?"

Tara's laughter rang out. "So there are kisses for different times of the day?"

"There's no rule against that, milady."

She chuckled and shook her head in disbelief. "Alright, permission granted. You may go ahead."

And Rex did just that, and he gave her a sweet mix of soft gentle kisses and hard, breath-stealing ones, pouring out all his affection into letting her know how much he'd come to adore her, this woman he'd initially misjudged, and who was perfect just the way she was.

Finally, they came up for air.

"Would you like more, milady?" Rex asked.

Tara swatted him on the chest. "You wish."

Rex chuckled and pulled her close to his heart.

Tara fitted into him like she belonged there. He let out a sigh of contentment.

"Tara?" he said after a while.

"Hmm?"

"Would you like to attend a charity event with me in Boston? It's next week, on Saturday." Weston had informed Rex about the auction, which was focused on raising funds for the rehabilitation of wounded horses, a matter close to Rex and his partners' hearts. They had also decided it was a good way to make new connections while contributing to a worthy cause. Weston, Liam, and Cole would be there.

"I'd love to go," Tara said. "But I don't think I have anything here to wear."

"I'll take care of that," he said.

"Okay."

Besides, Rex couldn't wait to introduce Tara as his girlfriend to the guys.

# CHAPTER 37

**R**ex stepped into the chandelier-filled ballroom with Tara on his arm. She looked stunning in a cap-sleeved grey gown with threads of silver running through it that shimmered with her every move. Matching diamond accessories completed her look. It felt great to have the most beautiful woman in the room by his side.

"Have I told you how gorgeous you look?" he said softly as they wound their way through the crowd to where Weston, Liam, and Cole waited. The guys had brought no dates.

Tara gave him a warm smile. "Like the tenth time, but you can keep telling me. I don't mind."

"I'm sure every guy wishes they were me," he

said as he noted the look of envy on some of the men's faces when they passed.

"Are you sure they're not mad at you because their ladies all want to be on your arm?"

The corners of Rex's lips turned up. "You're good for my ego, Tara," he said in a low voice.

"Say my name again."

"You look stunning, Tara."

Tara fought to hide her grin. "You'll be the death of me soon with that low, sexy voice of yours."

"Thank you, my darling. I aim to please."

By now they'd reached where the guys stood. It was a black-tie event, so they were all dressed in tuxedos. Rex noticed Liam's eyes widened at the sight of her.

"Hello," Tara said cheerily.

Cole's eyes swept over her from head to toe. "Tara, you look gorgeous," he said. "Like an oasis of water to a man dying of thirst." Weston bumped Cole's shoulder. "What?"

"Thank you, Cole," Tara said with a bemused smile.

"You're welcome," Cole responded. He turned to Weston. "See?"

"You look stunning, Tara," Liam said.

"I concur," Weston said. "Rex, you're one lucky man to have such a beautiful woman by your side."

"Absolutely," Rex said. "Weston, Liam, and Cole, please meet Tara, my beautiful, amazing girlfriend."

"Girlfriend?" they all said as one, their faces showing various degrees of shock.

Weston was the first to find his voice. "Rex, you old dog!" He clapped him on the shoulder. "So that's what you've been up to when you tell me you've been busy."

"What can I say? I'm a lucky man, Wes."

"That you are," Liam said, a little put out. But Rex was sure he'd be alright eventually.

"So when did this happen?" Cole asked.

"Recently," Rex said.

"You look happy," Weston said. "Relaxed and happy. Tara, please keep doing whatever you're doing that's made him like this. I'll forever be grateful to you."

Tara's eyes met Rex's, and she winked. "I'll try," she said. Rex was sure the kisses had crossed her mind.

Rex couldn't get enough of them. But more than that, Tara understood him. He didn't have to be anyone else but Rex. And he was enjoying getting to know her likes and dislikes, as well as her cute little quirks.

And they didn't have to talk all the time. Tara had come over a few times during the past week, and all they'd done was read—she her medical journals, and him his books on horses and ranch management, since they both liked to stay on top of the latest trends in their respective industries. In all cases, they did whatever was comfortable for both of them.

Tara had also not given up on riding and could now take the horse at as fast as a canter around the fenced area. Rex liked that about her—her ability and patience to persist in whatever she'd set her mind to do, even if she wasn't good at it at first. He had to admit he was smitten with her.

Rex gave her a kiss on the top of her head.

"Ugh, no public PDA," Cole said. "It's unhealthy for us single bachelors."

"Then maybe you should un-bachelor yourself," Rex said.

"No thanks," Cole said as if it was the most distasteful suggestion ever.

"I think the organizers are about to make a speech," Liam said, gesturing to the erected stage, and everyone turned in that direction.

"Good evening, ladies and gentlemen," a lady in

a purple dress with her hair piled on top of her head said. "Welcome to the Wounded Stables charity event, and thank you all for coming. Tonight, we'll be holding a charity auction to raise rehabilitation funds for injured horses. But first we'd like the sponsors of this event to give us a quick speech. Please welcome Mr. and Mrs. Carriford to the stage." A smattering of applause followed.

Tara stiffened beside him.

# CHAPTER 38

ara took a step back. No, it couldn't be. There had to be a million Carrifords all over the country. Besides, William's family had hailed from New York. What could they possibly be doing organizing an event in Boston?

But then the couple came up on stage, and Tara's knees almost buckled. She'd seen a picture of William's parents with him once in the newspaper, and now the same couple, albeit older, stood a few feet away from her.

Her chest tightened. *No!* It had to be a dream.

"Are you okay?" Rex asked from beside her.

But she couldn't really hear him. Just when she finally had something great happening in her life, this family from hell had to show up to snatch her joy away.

Then another lady joined the couple on stage, and Tara's breath hitched.

How could this be? Though she looked older and more sophisticated, Tara would have recognized her anywhere.

Her former roommate, Catherine.

With the Carrifords.

And then the speaker introduced her as William's wife.

Tara's heart hammered. Catherine, her best friend in high school, had married Tara's rapist.

She'd always assumed Catherine had revealed the information about the barn under duress. But now it seemed she'd done it for more—for a place at William's side. Catherine had traded her friend for wealth and power.

Tara couldn't think. She had to go, though she had no idea where. She just needed a place to breathe, away from these ugly, horrible people.

So she turned and fled the room.

# CHAPTER 39

"*T*ara, wait!" Rex called after her, but she ignored him and hurried in the direction of the exit.

Rex went after her. What was going on? This was unlike Tara. But the look he'd seen in her eyes told him something horrible had happened.

Rex had never seen her look so scared, not even when she'd climbed onto the horse for the first time. Something must have spooked her, and Rex needed to protect her.

He rushed after her through the crowd, but by the time he'd reached the doors, Tara was nowhere to be seen.

Rex's pulse raced. Where could she be? Rex had never been scared since Tammy died, not even when a bucking horse had almost thrown him off. But he was afraid now. He had to find Tara.

He checked the rooms near the ballroom on either side of the hallway, but there was no Tara in them. Rex looked into the other rooms as he moved down the hallway, but he still found no sign of her. He soon reached the last room and peered in. Tara was nowhere to be seen. By now, Rex was frightened out of his mind. *God, please help me find her*, he prayed silently.

Then he heard a sniffle and then another. It was coming from the opposite room, one he'd already checked. Rex burst in and looked around. It was a large conference room, and at first it appeared empty.

Then he heard the sniffling again. This time, it was closer. Rex followed the sound until he reached the other end of the table and looked down.

Tara crouched there with a hand over her mouth.

Thank God he'd found her.

Rex went down slowly on his knees so as not to scare her. "Are you okay?" he asked softly.

She looked up at him with tears streaming down her eyes.

Rex's chest tightened, and his anger began to boil. He wanted to hurt whoever had made Tara cry.

But he couldn't let her see his fury—she needed

him. So he reached out gently and pulled her into his arms. "Shh, it's okay," he said as he rubbed her back gently.

Tara continued to sob, soaking his jacket with tears.

Rex's heart broke as he continued to comfort her. Someone had hurt Tara, and that person would pay.

Eventually, her weeping slowed and then stopped.

Rex retrieved a hanky from his pocket and handed it to her.

"Thank you," Tara said as she accepted it. "I know I must look a sight."

He pressed a kiss on her forehead. "You look beautiful as always," he said.

Tara let out a shaky laugh. "Only you would say that."

"Do you want to talk about it?" he asked softly.

She nodded. "I'd like to sit against the wall."

Rex released her, and she adjusted until her back rested on the wall. Rex did the same. Then he waited for her until she was ready.

"In my sophomore year of high school, I was raped."

Rex's heart slammed against his rib cage like a hammer against a rock. It was the last thing he'd expected to hear, and he already detested the monster who'd done it.

His hand clenched into a tight fist as he listened to how a fellow student of hers had bullied, trapped, and then abused her—and how his parents and the school had covered up the crime. Rex fought the urge to punch the wall. He considered men who rape as the bottom of the barrel and the worst of men. This evil monster had brutalized Tara.

Just like what had happened to Rose.

And he'd considered the Carriford family as a potential business partner because of their extensive interests in horses.

Rex hated himself in that moment. Even though he hadn't known about the rape, he'd exposed Tara to the trauma again. "I'm so sorry, Tara."

"It's not your fault," she said. "William was the devil, not you."

"I shouldn't have brought you here."

"It's alright. You didn't know. We were bound to meet again one way or the other."

"And the bastard is dead." Rex had read about William's death in the profile Weston had put together about the Carriford family.

Her eyes registered shock at his words. "Really?" It was clear she hadn't known. "I'm glad he's dead."

"I wish he wasn't."

Tara looked at him in surprise. "Why?"

"I would have sent him to the grave myself."

Tara gave him a small smile. "I know you wouldn't—you're not a violent man—but thanks for saying that. It means a lot to me." She folded the hanky in her hands. "So that's me, who I am."

"Look at me," Rex said. Tara locked eyes with him. "What you've told me doesn't change how I feel about you. Quite the opposite. I'm proud of you for pulling your life back together again and making a success of it. Because you, Tara, are a success. You're beautiful, smart, funny, and a wonderful radiologist." At her arched eyebrow, "Zoey told me."

Tara laughed, a warm sound Rex was glad to hear. He'd been afraid it'd be gone for a while.

"Don't believe everything Zoey tells you," she said. Then her face turned serious. "I didn't do it alone. Succeed, I mean. I had help from a few wonderful folks along the way. But thank you for saying that."

"You're welcome." He brushed her hair away from her face. "Would you like to leave now?"

She thought for a moment. "Not yet. I'd like to meet his widow."

# CHAPTER 40

Tara made her way through the packed ballroom with Rex by her side. She'd freshened up in the bathroom and now held her head high as she scanned the room for Catherine. The series of speeches had finished, and the auction was expected to begin shortly. Tara hoped to speak with her before it started.

She spotted her in a far corner of the room chatting with an elderly couple. Tara moved through the crowd until she reached her.

"Catherine," Tara said. There was no way she was calling her by her last name.

Catherine turned. "Hello! Do I know you?" she asked. Then her eyes widened in surprise and then fear as she recognized Tara.

"I'm Tara. Nice to meet you," she said. Rose was dead, and she never wanted to be called by that name again.

"Hello, Tara," Catherine managed to say. She turned to the couple. "I'm sorry, will you excuse me?" The couple drifted away. Then her eyes met Tara's. "Fancy meeting you here." She seemed to have recovered herself.

But Tara wasn't fooled. "Every so often, I've thought about you, Catherine, but I had no idea you were a backstabber. Did it feel good betraying your friend for money?"

Catherine's eyes darted around as if hoping no one else had heard the words. "Now, look—"

"Once a rapist, always a rapist," Tara interjected. She leaned closer. "Your life must have been so sad, Catherine."

Catherine's face remained a stoic mask, but Tara saw the muscle in her jaw twitch. She'd hit a nerve.

"Don't worry. I won't out you," Tara continued. "But I hope for your sake our paths never cross again. Goodbye, Catherine."

Tara swiveled and left, heading straight for the exit.

"You did great," Rex said from beside her.

She'd forgotten he was there. "Thanks. I'd like to leave now."

"Your wish is my command," Rex said.

# CHAPTER 41

Rex dropped Tara at the main house and then placed a call to Zoey, letting her know her friend needed her. Zoey promised to be there shortly.

But now he needed to take care of another important matter. Maybe this was why he'd met Tara—an opportunity to redeem himself for what had happened with Rose. A second chance to make things right. He would not fail this time.

Rex returned to his place to see Weston, Liam, and Cole already waiting at his front door.

"What is it, Rex?" Weston said as Rex led them into the living room. "I'm sure you have a good reason for pulling us out of the charity auction."

"Don't worry," Rex said. "We'll send our donation directly to Wounded Stables."

"What's going on?" Liam said as they all settled on the couch. "We got your emergency message and came immediately."

"I need your help," Rex said without preamble.

"You know we'll help in whatever way we can," Cole said.

"I need to seek justice for someone."

"Who?" Weston asked.

"For Tara." Rex didn't go into detail. It wasn't his story to tell.

Liam leaned forward. "Tell us what you need us to do."

# CHAPTER 42

Tara woke up with a mild headache. She'd cried again last night after Zoey had shown up. They'd talked for a long time before finally falling asleep in the early hours of the morning. But the spot beside her was now empty, so Zoey must have left at some point.

She reached for her phone and grimaced at the time on the screen. It was already mid-morning—way past the time she was supposed to have taken care of the horses with Rex. She'd also missed church. But there was a message from Rex, telling her not to worry about helping with the horses if she wasn't feeling up to it.

Tara smiled to herself. The man got her. Yesterday would have been a disaster if Rex hadn't been there. But she was glad that was over—she'd never cry about that incident again.

Then the smell of coffee hit her nose.

Tara tracked the scent to the door and opened it. A service table stood right outside, with fresh flowers and a note on it. She picked up the note and opened it. It read:

"Fresh coffee for you, milady, just the way you like it. R."

A smile teased her lips as she picked up the flowers and pressed them against her nose. She loved the way Rex kept surprising her. Who would have imagined he'd pick flowers for her?

And how had Rex managed to get the table up the stairs? And he'd missed church too. He must have stayed back to take care of her. He was too good to her.

She replaced the flowers and wheeled the table into her room. Soon, Tara dove into the hot breakfast that had accompanied the coffee, which she saved for last.

Finally, she took a sip of the coffee and sighed happily. Rex had prepared it just the way she liked it, and by the time Tara had finished the cup, she felt much better. She replaced the plates on the service table and pushed it back out the room. She'd take it down after she'd freshened up.

Tara took a shower in the luxurious bathroom, and then dressed in a cream blouse and jeans. But when she opened the door to take care of the service table, it was gone. Rex must have removed it while she was in the shower, so she grabbed her phone and sent him a text.

**Tara: Thanks for breakfast! ::heart emoji::**

**Rex: You're welcome. ::smile emoji:: Try and rest as much as you can.**

**Tara: Will do my best.**

**Rex: I'll see you later.**

**Tara: Bye! ::heart emoji::**

Since it was too late to join the service in Dexin, Tara connected to the online service of her home church. Fortunately, it was just beginning, so she joined the service for the next two hours. By the time it was over, Tara felt refreshed. She pulled out her laptop and then worked on her research for the next hour. Every little bit of time she spent on it helped, as Tara hoped to have it ready in time for the annual national radiology conference a few months away.

Once she was satisfied with her progress, she closed her laptop and stretched her limbs. Maybe it was time for a nap.

Her phone rang, and she picked it up. "This is Tara Ellis."

"Tara, it's Larry." Larry was Hyacinth's nephew, and he'd become a close friend. He was a juvenile lawyer in New York City.

"Hey, Larry. What's up?"

"It's Hailey," Larry said in a grave voice. "She's in trouble."

Tara's phone slipped out of her hands and clattered to the floor.

CHAPTER 43

Tara scrambled to pick up her phone even as her mind raced.

Hailey was Tara's daughter—who she'd given up for adoption.

The couple who'd adopted her had requested a closed adoption, and Tara had agreed. She'd wanted no chance of the Carrifords tracking down Hailey if they found out she'd had William's baby. But it meant Tara had no direct access to her. Fortunately, she'd had a backup plan and had tracked down the couple's identity.

Tara had never approached the couple or Hailey, but she'd had Larry keep an eye on Hailey and requested that he only update Tara if there was anything amiss. So far, the couple had loved and treated Hailey well, so there'd been no news.

But now, Hailey was in trouble. What had happened?

"I'm sorry, the phone slipped out of my hand," Tara said. Fortunately, the screen wasn't broken. "You were saying?"

"You need to come to New York, Tara."

"Is Hailey okay?" That was the most important question.

"Her parents passed away two weeks ago, and she's in juvie."

Tara's heart ached at the news. Hailey must be devastated by the loss. And juvie? She'd never been the kind to court trouble. Something must be wrong. "How did I not hear about this?" she said as she opened the closet and reached for her purse and a pair of comfortable shoes.

"I was still on my annual vacation when it happened," Larry said. "I only got back yesterday to meet this. Sorry about that."

"No worries. I know you've always done your best wherever Hailey is concerned." She donned her shoes. "I'll be right there as soon as I can." Tara ended the call.

That was when she remembered she had no car.

She would have to ask Rex. But then she'd have to tell him she had a daughter from the rape incident, and she wasn't ready for that conversation. Tara had to find another way.

She dialed Zoey's number, and she picked up on the first ring. "Hey, what's going on?"

"I need a car. I have to go up to New York, but I'll be back later today."

"You can take mine. It's parked in front of the main house, since I rode with Dex to church. The key is on the hook by the door."

"Thanks."

"Anytime."

Tara ended the call, grabbed her purse, and hurried out of her room and down the stairs. Thankfully, there was no one in the living room or kitchen. Everyone was probably at church. Well, except Rex. She found Zoey's key and raced outside.

And slammed into a well-built chest. Tara looked up to see Rex in a blue shirt and jeans.

"Why the hurry? Is everything okay?" Rex asked, his eyes searching hers.

"I need to be in New York."

"I'll take you."

"Aren't you busy?"

"Not for you. And the SUV would be faster than taking Zoey's car."

"How did you know I was taking Zoey's vehicle?"

"The keychain with the Mini Cooper logo. I've seen Zoey with it before."

"Oh." She looked down at her hand and saw what he meant. She hadn't even noticed.

Tara didn't want to take Rex with her, but maybe she didn't have to tell him who the girl was to her. And Rex's car would indeed be faster. "Let me return Zoey's keys, and we can get going," she said.

Soon they were in the SUV and on their way to New York. After a few minutes into the ride, Tara turned to Rex. "You're not asking," she said.

"About why you need to go to New York? I figured you'd tell me whenever you're ready."

"I'm not sure I'll ever be ready."

"That works too. Just let me know what address we need to go to once we get closer to New York."

"Okay."

The drive took over two hours. Tara stayed silent —all she could think about was Hailey. But she prayed and prayed that everything would turn out alright.

Once they neared New York, Tara called Larry. "Where do you want me to meet you?" she asked.

"At the juvie center." He gave her the address, which she repeated for Rex.

Rex didn't bat an eyelid and just inputted the information into his GPS. They arrived at the location thirty minutes later.

Though he'd checked out the sign as he parked in front of the building, Rex still had said nothing. He hopped out instead and opened the door for her.

"Go on. I'll be waiting," Rex said after she'd stepped down.

"Are you sure?"

"Positive." He gave her a hug and then released her.

# CHAPTER 44

Rex watched as Tara walked away, then he got back into the car.

What could Tara be possibly doing at a juvenile detention center? Was a friend's child or a mentee in trouble? Rex hoped whoever it was would be okay.

He would have loved to offer his support, but he'd promised to wait until she was ready to share what was going on.

So Rex pushed his seat backward, closed his eyes, and settled in to wait.

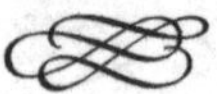

# CHAPTER 45

Tara strode over to a brown sedan and knocked on the driver's window.

The glass slid down, and a close-shaven head poked out.

"Hello, Larry," Tara said.

"Tara." The driver's door opened, and a tall young man in a tweed jacket stepped out. "How was your trip?"

"Good. What happened?"

"Hailey was arrested for theft of stolen jewelry. The case was filed after her father's sister reported the jewelry stolen. The cops found the items in Hailey's jacket."

Tara crossed her arms over her chest. "Why do I smell a rat? Hailey's parents were well-off."

"More than well-off. They owned a clothing store that's worth about a million dollars."

"And this is her first offense, yet she's in juvie instead of being on probation?"

"Correct."

"Who's her guardian on record now that her parents are dead?" Tara asked.

"The same aunt."

"So she must have found out how much Hailey is worth and wants all that money for herself. Maybe a setup?"

"That's what I'm thinking."

"But locking her up in juvie doesn't eliminate Hailey's right to the inheritance."

Larry leaned against his car. "But it does give her aunt time to tamper with the money and property without Hailey's interference. And who knows what could happen in juvie?" He folded his arms across his chest. "And that's not all."

Tara groaned. "More bad news?"

"The aunt wants to put her into foster care."

That was indeed terrible news. "We need to get her out."

"Correct."

"She has a court-appointed lawyer, right?"

"Yep. Fresh out of law school, and pretty green."

"Yikes. I'd like you to be her lawyer and take over her case," Tara said.

"I guessed you'd want that, and that's why we're here," Larry stated. "I have to get her consent to represent her, even if I won't be able to do a fee contract with her."

"That's fine. You know I'll handle all the legal fees."

"I already assumed that. Let me go in and speak with her, and I'll let you know what she says. You can wait in my car." He grabbed his slim briefcase and handed her the car keys.

"Alright."

Tara watched him pass through the gates of the juvie center. It would be a while, so she went back to Rex's car.

"Done so soon?" Rex asked.

"Not yet. We could be here a while. I have to go back and wait. Is that okay?"

"Sure."

Tara appreciated that he'd asked no further questions. "Thank you," she said.

"You're welcome," Rex replied. "Now go do what you need to. I'll be here."

"Won't you be bored?"

"I have a few calls to make, but I can do that from

the car. Otherwise, a nap never hurts." Tara chuckled. "There you go. I needed to see that smile." He placed his hand over hers. "Whatever it is, everything will work out fine."

Tara kissed him on the cheek. What had she done to deserve this wonderful man? "Thanks for the encouragement."

Rex gave her a warm smile. "Now go."

Tara left him and returned to wait by Larry's car.

Thirty minutes later, Larry was out.

Tara rushed to him. "How is she? What did she say?"

Larry held up a hand. "One question at a time. She seems okay. Appears to be taking it in stride." He walked to where his car was parked and leaned against it. "But she wants to see the legal ID of the person who hired me before she agrees. I told her I'd have to check with my client."

"She's one smart cookie."

"Well, she's your child, so I'm not surprised. I think she wants to be sure I wasn't hired by her aunt to screw her over. So what do you want to do?"

"Give it to her." Tara retrieved her driver's license from her wallet and handed it over to Larry.

"What if this backfires later, since you're not

supposed to contact her per the rules of the closed adoption?"

"I didn't contact her directly," Tara pointed out. "And she's the one requesting the information."

"Okay. But don't say I didn't warn you. You know what? I'll take a picture of your license instead. I'd rather she didn't know you were here." He took a snapshot of her license with his phone and handed it back to her.

"Thanks. Now go."

Larry straightened. "I'm going. I'm going."

Tara mused over Hailey's request. Contrary to Larry's assumption, Tara believed there might be another possible reason. Had Hailey found out who her biological mother was and wanted to confirm she was the one that had hired the lawyer?

She pinched the bridge of her nose. Maybe she was reading too much meaning into this.

Larry returned after a while and soon reached where Tara stood.

"How did it go?" Tara asked.

"She took one look at your license and said yes."

"Do you think she recognized me?"

Larry thought for a moment. "I'm not sure. She only said you seemed like an honest person from your photo."

"That was all?"

"She wants us to get her released into your care. She doesn't want foster care or her aunt's place."

"Can we make that happen?"

"It's a tricky one, since there's no history of any interaction of any form between you two, and you're not related to her—well, not on paper. But it's possible. However, you'll need to come back to New York. They'll likely want home visits and background checks before she can be released into your care."

Tara's mind began to spin. "Would it be possible for me to become her foster parent, even though I'm single?"

"Sure. You have no criminal record, you earn good money, and you'd need to be certified. But the fact that you work shifts might work against you. They'd want to know who would be watching over her while you are out for a night shift or for an emergency."

"I only work a few hours at a time as an attending, but I can always hire a nanny if needed," Tara said. "I've saved enough over the years to be able to afford that. If push comes to shove, I could switch to full-time research as a last resort."

"Okay, that's good to know. Besides that, the process can be slow moving, and anyone can file to adopt her during that time. Your best bet is to push for a private adoption from the outset. That's what I'd recommend."

And Tara agreed. Hailey needed her, and there was no way Tara was going to leave her in the hands of the state.

But what about Rex? Going out with her was one thing, but a daughter? Tara couldn't force him to accept her.

For Tara, Hailey was her first priority. She'd failed her once before, and Tara couldn't do it again.

Which left her with only one option. And another decision she loathed to make.

What was she going to do?

# CHAPTER 46

Rex studied Tara as she returned to the SUV. Her shoulders had slumped. Maybe whatever she'd come to do hadn't worked out.

He hopped out and opened the front passenger door for her. "Did everything go well?" he asked.

"It did."

"So what's with the long face?"

"I'm just tired." She really did look it.

"Okay," Rex said. "Where are we going next?"

"Back to Dexin."

"Alright."

Rex got in and backed out of the parking lot. Soon they were on the highway, and fortunately, there wasn't much traffic.

He glanced at Tara. From her demeanor, something appeared amiss. But what could it be? Though it stung that she didn't feel comfortable sharing what was on her mind with him, Rex reminded himself he'd promised to wait until she was ready to reveal what was going on.

A few hours later, they were back in Dexin and in front of the main house. Tara had been silent the whole ride.

Rex turned to her. "Is there anything I can do for you?"

Tara gave him a strained smile. "I'm just tired."

Rex didn't think that was it, but he didn't push. "Try and get some rest, okay?" She nodded.

He got out and then opened the door for her. When she exited, Rex wrapped his arms around her, and Tara held tight onto him, clinging to him as if afraid to let go.

Rex's brow furrowed. What had happened? Still, he'd would wait until she was ready to open up to him and could only reassure her in the meantime.

"I'll be here for you," he said. "Just call if you need me."

They stayed that way for a while. Then Rex released her.

He couldn't help worrying as Tara trudged up the

front steps, entered, and closed the door behind her. She never turned back to either look at him or wave goodnight.

It seemed something bad was about to happen, and Rex was powerless to stop it.

# CHAPTER 47

Tara collapsed on the bed and curled herself into a ball. How was she going to break the news to Rex? Her heart was heavy just thinking about it.

Rex was wonderful for her, and even though they'd only known each other for a short time, Tara couldn't imagine life without him. Yet she had to break his heart no matter how much it hurt.

What choice did she have?

Bringing a boyfriend into the picture would only complicate the adoption process, and she couldn't jeopardize the chance of successfully adopting Hailey. Hailey deserved her all, and it was important to provide her a feeling of security and belonging, especially after the loss of her parents.

But Tara would miss Rex. He'd burrowed his way into her heart and made her feel like she was the most important person in his world. And his family was awesome—they were like the family she'd never had but wished she did, and she felt right at home with them. Yet Tara wasn't sure they'd be able to accept Hailey, and she wasn't willing to risk it—the last thing her daughter needed was yet another rejection.

Most importantly, Tara didn't have the courage to face Rex.

So how was she going to handle this?

# CHAPTER 48

Rex heard a banging on his front door from the garage, where he'd been working on the vintage truck. He'd finally removed the car cover and had started spending a few hours each morning, after he was done with his chores, refamiliarizing himself with the restoration process.

He dropped the tools he'd been using back in their designated spots, removed his gloves, and headed into the living room. Who could it possibly be?

Rex opened the door to see Dex and Zoey standing on his front steps.

"What did you do to her?" Zoey said with an accusing glare.

Rex looked from Zoey to Dex in confusion. He

didn't understand what she'd just said. "What's going on?"

"Tara's gone, Rex," Dex said. "She left a note saying she was on her way back to New York."

"Wait. Hold on. What are you talking about?"

"She just left. And that's unlike her," Zoey said in a panicked tone.

"That's not possible. I was with her yesterday…" Then he remembered how unhappy she'd looked.

"What is it?" Dex asked.

Rex ignored him and instead rushed to his bedroom to look for his phone.

It couldn't be. There was no way she'd leave without telling him.

But where was his phone?

He found it on the nightstand. A light blinked, indicating an unread message, and he opened it.

**Tara: I'm sorry, Rex. There can't be anything between us. I have to go back to New York. Goodbye.**

Rex slumped on the bed. *No!* This couldn't be happening. How could Tara just break up with him like that? His heart hurt like it had been slashed open with a hot knife.

"What happened?" Dex asked.

Rex looked up. He hadn't even noticed they'd followed him into the bedroom.

"She broke up with me. Via text." He shook his head. "This can't be happening."

"So you didn't do anything to her?" Zoey asked.

"I love her!" Rex ran his hands through his hair. Yes, he loved her. He hadn't been sure before, but he was now.

And Rex was certain Tara cared for him. She couldn't just break up with him unless…

It must have something to do with yesterday's events. Maybe Tara thought he'd never love or accept her if he knew what it was. Because he was sure Tara wasn't the type to lead people on.

But Rex would go through fire for her—she was that precious. He didn't care about her secrets—he knew her heart. So maybe she just needed to understand he loved her no matter what and would always be there for her.

He sprang to his feet. "I need to go."

"Where are you going?" Dex asked.

"To find her. I think something happened yesterday in New York that has her scared. I need to let her know I'll always be by her side no matter what."

"I'm proud of you, Rex," Dex said, placing a hand on his shoulder. "Go get her."

"I'll text you her address," Zoey said, pulling out her phone. "I'm sorry I attacked you."

"You were only worried about her," Rex said. "This time I think I'll need all the prayers I can get."

"We'll be praying," Dex reassured him. "Now go."

Rex grabbed his wallet and his car keys, donned his boots, and sprinted out of the house.

It was time to bring his love, the woman of his heart, back home.

## CHAPTER 49

ara unbolted the front door of her brownstone to find Rex standing on the other side.

"What are you doing here?" she forced herself to say coldly. She couldn't allow herself to soften at the sight of him, even though all she wanted to do was fall into his arms.

"May I come in?" he said.

It wasn't a good idea to let him, but the thought of turning him away like that made her heart ache.

She opened the door wider and let him in—Rex had to duck his head to make it through.

"You may sit," Tara said, motioning to the only couch in the space. She settled into a high-backed chair opposite him. Any closer and she would weaken.

"Nice place," Rex said, looking around.

Tara couldn't help feeling pleasure at his words. She'd furnished her home in vibrant jewel colors which were still her, in contrast with the muted colors she liked to wear. But she had to get him out of here as fast as she could—any longer and the walls she'd just erected around her heart again could come crashing down.

"What are you doing here?" she asked.

Rex locked eyes with her, the warmth in them pulling her in against her will. "I love you, Tara."

Tara froze. He loved her? Her heart fluttered in excitement, but she tamped down the joy that tried to bloom there. "It's over, Rex."

Rex leaned forward. "I'm not sure you understand what I just said. I love you, Tara, no matter your secrets or whatever was troubling you yesterday. I love you no matter what, and I'll never leave you."

Tara's heart raced. Could she believe it? No, he wouldn't love her if he found out she had a daughter, and not just any, but her rapist's. And she couldn't allow anything to affect Hailey's adoption process.

"It's too late, Rex."

Rex got up and then knelt, placing his hands on

the arms of her chair and caging her in. "I love you, Tara, no matter what."

She shook her head. "No, Rex." His nearness was eroding her resolve.

"Try me."

"I have a daughter!"

His eyes widened for a moment. But then he said. "Okay."

"Okay?"

"It's an unexpected surprise, but it makes no difference to me. It only means you and she are a package deal, which is fine with me. So when do I meet her?"

"You don't understand, Rex. Hailey is my daughter from the rape!"

There was a moment of silence. Tara wasn't sure how Rex would react.

Then he touched her chin, the action sending sparks of electricity through her skin. "It doesn't matter, Tara. She's your daughter, but more than that, she's God's daughter. Thankfully, that bastard is dead, and his parental rights no longer exist. So what's the problem?"

"I can't leave her behind."

"So I'll adopt her."

"You don't understand. I'm just starting the

process myself. I gave her up for adoption, can't you see? I failed her once, but now she needs me." Tara told him about Hailey's situation. "I can't have anything holding up the adoption process, Rex. Dating you might do that."

"So marry me."

# CHAPTER 50

*R*ex couldn't believe he'd just said that, but he meant every word. He couldn't imagine life without Tara. Interestingly, the thought of a new daughter didn't scare him either. Sure, he had no experience in that department, but he would learn as much as he could about it. Besides, he had a wonderful family behind him that would help.

"Please don't joke about this," Tara said.

"I'm serious, Tara. I'll marry you today, tomorrow, or next week if you want. Being married will help the adoption process, and we can provide all the extra support Hailey needs. Tara, I'm with you on this journey for the long haul. Would you be willing to jump in with me?"

"Is that a proposal?"

"Hold on." He jumped to his feet and grabbed the fake flowers he'd spotted in a vase on the kitchen countertop. Rex also removed a brass college ring he'd always worn and then dropped to one knee. "Tara Ellis, the captor of my heart, will you marry me?" He held out the flowers in his left hand and the brass ring on his right.

"This is ridiculous."

"But you love me all the same. Marry me, Tara," Rex said in that low voice she loved.

He could see her resolve weakening at his words. "Are you sure?" she asked.

Rex nodded. He was in it until 'death do us part.'

"You can't back out."

"I know. It's non-refundable."

Tara chuckled, and her face relaxed. "Yes, I'll marry you, Rex Dexin."

A smile spread across his face. She'd said yes. He dropped the flowers and wrapped her into a tight hug. "Yes!"

"Rex, I can't breathe."

He released her. "Sorry."

"Aren't you forgetting something?"

"What? Oh, the ring." He slipped it onto her ring finger, but it came right off. "It's too big." He should have gotten a ring on his way, but who knew he'd propose?

"I have a solution." She slipped it onto her thumb. "There."

Rex kissed the ring on her finger and then looked up. They were each other's from now on. "I love you, Tara," he said solemnly.

Tears filled her eyes. "Thank you."

Then he gave her a soft tender kiss he hoped would reassure her that she was treasured and loved just the way she was, and that everything would turn out alright.

Now he had to break the news to his family.

"Is this a joke?" Max said to Rex. The family had all gathered in the living room, and Rex had just broken the news to them.

"No," Rex said firmly. "Tara and I are getting married next week."

"But why the rush?" Maggie asked. "You just started dating."

"I'm sure he has a good reason," Peter said. Rex appreciated the vote of confidence, but the truth was Tara's secret to share, not his. He had to protect her.

"It's just how it is," Rex said. "But it's for a good reason, and I'd love it if you could just trust me on this."

"Is this another impulse decision?" Max said.

"Hey, that was uncalled for," Rex said. "And it's not like we're having a Vegas wedding." It was a dig at Max, who'd met Becca in Vegas one evening and married her the same night, though they'd both been drugged by Max's stalker at the time.

"I'm sorry," Max said as he rubbed his forehead. "This is just so sudden. I'm not sure I can support that."

Rex deflated. Of course he was still going to marry Tara no matter what, but he would have loved to have his family behind him.

"Rex and Tara, can I speak to you for a minute?" Maggie said. "Come."

They followed her into Maggie's old bedroom. Maggie and Peter now had a home of their own on the property, but she still liked to use the place whenever she was in the main house. She pointed to the bed with the quilted comforter. "Sit."

Rex and Tara sat side by side, and Rex gave her an encouraging smile.

"Tell me what's going on," Maggie said.

"Maggie," Tara started.

Rex grabbed her arm. "You don't have to say it."

Tara patted his hand. "I do. I don't want any misunderstandings between you and your family. Let me protect you." She smiled back at him.

This right here was why he couldn't help falling in love with her. "Okay."

Tara turned back to Maggie. "I have a daughter. Hailey." Then Tara told her the whole story. "I need to adopt her, and dating Rex won't look good right now."

"And instead of breaking up with her, I'd rather marry her," Rex finished.

"Okay. Thanks for telling me the details. Rex, do you love her?"

"I do." This he was absolutely sure about.

"And Tara, do you love Rex, your daughter notwithstanding?"

Tara looked Maggie straight in the eye. "I never thought I'd find love again. I didn't think I deserved it after giving up my child for adoption. But Rex made me wish for it. I know you're worried about him, but I'd never hurt him. He has my heart."

Maggie visibly relaxed. "Alright, but you need to tell the family why you need to marry now. Not the details. Just that you need to bring your daughter home. Does that work?"

"I can do that," Tara said.

"Good. Let's get back before they drive each other up the wall with worry. And Tara?"

"Yes?"

"Welcome to the family." Maggie opened her arms and pulled Tara into a hug.

Rex's shoulders loosened. Everything was going to turn out just fine.

A few minutes later, Tara told the family why they were getting married so quickly as Maggie had suggested.

"You have a daughter?" Becca said. "Now Chloe has a playmate."

"She's sixteen," Rex said.

"Oh. Well, Chloe will have a big sister." There was a reason Becca had grown on Rex.

"And you love each other?" Max asked.

Rex held Tara's hand in his. "We do."

"I love him more than words can say," Tara said.

Rex's heart warmed at her words. Now how could he beat that?

"Okay," Max said. "Count me in."

Rex released an exhale. He'd needed Max's support the most.

"I didn't know," Zoey said.

Tara gave her a small smile. "I never told anyone."

Zoey got up and hugged her. "It must have been hard keeping that all to yourself."

'So you're getting yourself a daughter now?" Dex said to Rex. "I don't envy you, bro. I hope she's not another Chloe."

"Hey!" Becca said.

"What's wrong with my daughter?" Max said. "She's the best in the whole world."

Dex lifted his hands in surrender. "No offense, Becca, Max. Chloe is adorable. But two of *her* in the house? They'd run us ragged and have us wrapped around their little fingers."

Becca turned to Chloe, who'd been coloring a book on the coffee table. "Chloe, your Uncle Dex just insulted you," she said, ruffling her hair.

Chloe folded her arms over her chest and glared at Dex. "Uncle Dex, you get two pairs of orange socks."

"I'm sorry, Chloe. I didn't mean it," Dex said.

"Or maybe the kitten socks? They're lime green."

Dex winced as Rex fought to hold back a smile. "I'll take the orange socks. Thank you for your mercy, Your Highness."

Lime green? Rex would have dodged it too.

"Congratulations on the new daughter!" Peter said with a relaxed smile.

"Thank you, sir."

"Let me know if you need any help with the adoption process. I might know some people in New York who could be useful."

"Will do, sir."

"Oh, please call me Peter."

"So when do we meet Hailey?" Max asked.

"In a few days." Rex and Tara had agreed to bring her down to the ranch on her release, since they'd both be here and the environment and family support would do her good. Tara had introduced Rex to Larry, and Larry had assured them he'd make it happen.

But Rex wondered if Hailey would accept them.

# CHAPTER 51

Rex paced the edge of the helipad area as they waited for the helicopter bringing Tara and Hailey to arrive. What if Hailey didn't like him?

"She'll love you," Dex said as if he could read Rex's thoughts and squeezed his shoulder.

Larry had gotten Hailey released into Tara's care, and Max had sent his helicopter to pick them up from New York. The helicopter now made its way to them and soon landed on the helipad.

Rex waited for the blades to stop spinning, then he rushed forward and opened the door.

Tara came out first, then helped a younger girl alight after her.

Rex's heart went into overdrive, and he stilled.

Hailey looked like an older version of Rose. How was this possible?

"Rex?" Tara's voice brought him back to the present.

"Oh! Sorry." He smiled at Hailey. "I'm Rex Dexin. It's nice to meet you."

"Oh, Tara's fiancé. Got it," she said, her voice pleasant but reserved.

That didn't go so bad.

"And this is my brother, Dex."

Hailey looked up at Dex. "Are you all this tall?"

Dex chuckled. "Pretty much."

"Why don't we head to the house?" Tara said.

"I'll grab the bags," Rex said.

"I'll do it," Dex said to Rex. "You go ahead with the ladies."

Rex clapped his shoulder. "Thanks."

They reached the house, and Rex introduced Hailey to the rest of the family.

The family welcomed her wholeheartedly, with Maggie taking her immediately under her wing. Soon she had her smiling in the kitchen as they made cupcakes. Tara and Zoey helped as well.

But Rex couldn't forget how much she reminded him of Rose.

What if Rose wasn't dead like he'd thought? What if the woman who'd told him had been wrong?

Then Rex studied Tara. Sure, she had dark hair, but what if she'd dyed it? And she'd always felt somewhat familiar to him.

She took her coffee the same way Rose had told him she liked hers.

Tara had recognized the *Oliver Twist* book they'd both loved.

And she'd been attacked in high school like Rose had been. Tara had said she'd attended a local county high school. But what if she'd gone to the prestigious academy first and finished up at the local high school?

Rex's heart thudded in his chest. There were too many similarities to dismiss as mere coincidences. The practical thing to do was to hold on until the end of the day when Hailey had settled in for the night and then ask Tara about it.

But he couldn't wait. Rex had to know.

Rex reached Tara and pulled her aside. "Can I talk to you?"

"Can it wait?" She gestured at Hailey, who was focused on the cupcake she was decorating.

"It'll only be a few minutes."

Tara studied his face. "Okay," she said after a moment. "Hailey, I'll be right back."

Hailey looked up to see Rex. "Sure." Then she turned her attention back on what she'd been working on.

Rex led Tara outside and down all the way to the end of the driveway. He didn't need anyone eavesdropping on their conversation.

"What is it, Rex?" Tara said, her attention all focused on him.

"Did you attend a prestigious high school academy in upstate New York at any time?"

# CHAPTER 52

Tara stared at Rex. How did he know? "Yes."

"Have you ever been to Dexin before?" Rex asked.

Tara thought she might have mentioned it. "Yes." But why was he asking? "Rex, what's going on?"

"Were you ever called Rose?"

Tara froze. "Why do you ask?" Had he been digging into her background?

"Did you know Grandma Dee's corner store?"

"Rex?" Tara took a step back. No, there was no way Rex was Oliver. But Oliver was the only one who'd know all those details put together. The same Oliver who'd broken her heart. This couldn't be happening. Not now, when everything in her life was perfect.

Tara felt the urge to run as far away from here as possible, but she couldn't. She had a daughter who depended on her now. Tara couldn't hurt her again. She had to face this new complication head-on.

"Please just answer, Tara."

"Yes."

"Unbelievable." Rex ran his hands through his hair. "Rose, it's me, Oliver."

And just like that, the rug was pulled out from under Tara's feet. How had she ended up planning her life and that of her child around this man who'd hurt her? What was she going to do now? "I have to go," she said. She needed to go somewhere alone where she could think.

Rex put a hand on her arm. "Rose, please."

She whirled back. "I'm not Rose! Rose is dead!" Rose had been weak. Tara would never be like that again.

"Please, Tara, just listen."

"To excuses? Dear God, what did I do that was so horrible to deserve this joke? I fell in love with the man who broke my heart!"

He held onto her arm. "Please, Tara, just give me a few minutes to explain."

Tara wanted to just leave him like he'd left her, hurt him like he'd done to her. Yet a part of her wanted to hear the excuses so she could close this door firmly behind her with no regrets.

She brushed off his hand. "You have three minutes."

"Okay. I was on my way to pick you up when a truck ran into my vehicle. I woke up the next day in the hospital with a concussion and a broken leg. According to the doctors, it was a miracle that I made it out alive, and I was placed on mandatory bed rest."

He'd been in an accident? She hadn't known.

"I called you on the number you'd called the store with, but no one picked up on the other end," Rex continued.

"Yes, you wouldn't have been able to reach me at that number," Tara said. It had been the school barn's phone line.

"I called the school too, and they rejected my calls after they heard I was looking for you. I also wrote to you. And once I was able to, I got Max to bring me to your house in New York. But there was no one there, and your neighbor said you'd passed away."

Tara's eyebrows rose. She? Dead? It sounded ridiculous. "What neighbor?"

He thought for a moment. "I believe her name was Miss Whitaker. She said you'd died after an attack, and that your father had gone as well. You can ask Max to confirm what I've just told you. I'm sorry, Rose, I didn't mean to hurt you."

Tara was speechless for a moment. Miss Whitaker's confused mind had separated them? Who would have believed it?

She didn't know whether to laugh or cry. Still, she had to let him know how it'd been for her. "My heart broke when you didn't show up, Oliver."

"I'm sorry, Rose."

"I trusted you, and I felt let down. Like the world had abandoned me. And it hurt more than anything my father had ever done."

"I'm sorry, Rose." He pulled her into his arms. "I'll make it up to you for the rest of my life."

As she stayed in his arms, wrapped in his love, Tara was glad she'd listened to what he had to say. And it felt good to know that Oliver, the boy she'd loved and trusted, had never betrayed her. Instead, God had brought them back together again. "Thank you for looking for me then," she said. She glanced at his legs. "Does the leg still hurt?"

"It's fine," Rex reassured her. "It's as good as new now."

"I'm glad." She laid her head against his chest. "Thanks for telling me the truth. But how did you know?"

"When I saw Hailey. She looked like an older version of the Rose I first met. Then with the other clues—the way you take your coffee, the attack, the *Oliver Twist* book—everything fell into place."

"I thought you looked familiar the first time I saw you," Tara said. "And I wondered about the book, but I just figured it was a coincidence."

Rex brushed her hair away from her face. "But what happened to your dad?"

"He stayed with me at the hospital the whole time I was there, which was probably why Miss Whitaker never saw him. He passed away in my first year of college. Heart attack."

"I'm sorry."

Tara shrugged. "It was a long time ago."

Rex kissed her forehead. "One question though: why is your hair dark and short? It's one of the things that threw me off the Rose trail."

"I wanted nothing that reminded me of Rose. You don't like it?"

He gave her a light kiss on the lips. "I'm good with whatever makes you happy."

"Okay. Because I've grown used to this dark color."

"Either style suits you." He hugged her again. "Thank you, Rose, for coming back into my life."

"And it's Tara now."

"Noted." He tucked her hair behind her ear. "But remember, Rose was the spunky girl who first caught my eye, the one that had big dreams and loved greatly," he said softly. "The attack isn't all there is to her. She's an important piece of the best part of you, and she's still in here." He laid her hand over her heart. "But I'll try and abide by your wishes, Miss Tara Rose Ellis soon-to-be Dexin."

Tara pushed him away playfully and began to walk backwards. Her eyes twinkled. "Who said anything about changing my name?"

Rex followed her. "You don't want to?"

"Only if you can catch me." Tara took off running in the direction of the main house's entrance.

"Hey!" Rex raced after her.

Tara's laughter filled the air. She'd thought God had forgotten about her.

But he'd given her back her daughter and the boy who'd loved her.

EPILOGUE

Rex turned to Hailey as they stood in the midst of the flower garden on the ranch. Becca had helped create a very romantic, rustic-themed setting that still incorporated Tara's favorite jewel colors for the special occasion.

"Hailey, would you grant me permission to marry your mom, Tara Rose Ellis?" Rex asked.

"I thought you guys were already married," Hailey said. Tara and Rex had gotten married at city hall a few months ago, which had successfully aided in Hailey's adoption. But Rex wanted to give Tara the wedding she deserved. The proposal had been a surprise.

"Can you just play along?"

Hailey rolled her eyes, and Rex shook his head. What was it with teenagers and eye-rolling?

"Yes, you can marry Mom, whom you've already married."

Rex's lips turned up. Well, that was the best he could hope for. He loved this daughter of his, but the teenage years weren't exactly the easiest to deal with.

Then Rex turned to Tara and went down on one knee, the diamond ring he'd gotten for her in his hand. "Tara Rose Ellis, the love of my life, and the woman I adore. Would you marry me?" He'd love this woman until the day he died.

Tara's eyes shone with tears. "Yes, I will," she said.

Rex slid the ring on her finger and then rose to his feet and gave her a long kiss that spoke of all the love and happiness they shared, with more to come.

Clapping and shouts of *woohoo* filled the air, and they broke apart as his family and friends filled the space. The women chatted excitedly around Tara and admired her diamond ring with *oohs* and *aahs*.

Whatever was he going to do with his meddling family? They'd promised they'd stay out of it.

"Congrats, bro," Dex said. "You didn't really think we'd stay away, did you?"

Weston slapped his back. "That's the way to do

it." Rex and his partners had finally finished the renovations on the horse ranch. Rex planned to remain at Dexin Ranch, but Weston, Liam, and Cole would move into the DexGray Ranch.

"It'll be your turn next," Rex said.

"Not gonna happen. But it might with Jax." Weston motioned to where Jax stood close to a pretty lady Rex didn't recognize.

"Who's that?"

"Don't know. But Jax can't seem to take his eyes off her."

Rex could see that. Jax had been gone from the ranch for most of the time since Rex had come back home. He'd said it was for work, but Rex guessed it was because of him. There were still unresolved issues between him and Jax, and they'd only grown further apart since Rex returned. Jax had managed to be unavailable any time Rex wanted to meet with him. Still, Rex planned to make things right between them no matter what it took.

But for now, he was happy with his new family. Since they'd found each other, Rex and Tara had begged off the singles mixer event, and Miss Prissy had obliged. He'd heard the event had been a success, especially when Miss Prissy had informed attendees that the couple on the fliers had just gotten engaged.

Now she seemed to have more volunteers than she'd wished for, wanting to help out with future events. Dex had even told him that Jax had attended under threat from Maggie.

Since Tara had continued to work in New York, Rex had gotten a bigger house for their family close to the hospital where she was employed. Tara and Hailey lived there most of the time, while Rex commuted to Dexin instead. As a result, Tara hadn't been keeping up with her riding lessons, but that was sure to change, since Max had made her an employment offer at the ER Center, and she'd accepted.

Hailey had opted to take her GED instead. With Rex's help, she'd sold her adoptive parents' clothing store and had the money placed in a trust for her. She'd also told Tara how she'd found out about her after her parents died—they'd kept her adoption papers, and she'd found them while going through the memories they'd shared. She'd paid her a classmate with hacking skills to run a background check on Tara, so she'd recognized Tara once she'd seen the driver's license.

The Carrifords had found out about Hailey during the adoption process and attempted to fight for custody, since their son had never been convicted for the sexual crime. But Rex had put an end to that quickly by threatening to expose their son for the rapist he was. It turned out they valued their good name more than a potential granddaughter.

Per Rex's suggestion, the guys had informed Grandma Grayson on the type of people the Carrifords were—Rex and Weston had received an invite to the charity event due to that connection. Grandma Grayson had been furious and broken all relationships with the Carrifords, which had prompted other prominent Boston families to do the same, like Rex had anticipated, putting a halt to the Carrifords' planned expansion into Boston.

Liam and Cole had also hired a private investigator, who'd managed to find William's other victims. A few of them had banded together and filed a class action lawsuit against the Carrifords for aiding and abetting a rapist. Rex expected the Carrifords to be tied up in court for months to come. Tara and the other victims deserved justice for how the Carrifords had protected their son.

Even though Rex had experienced loss, God had given him much more than he'd deserved—bringing joy into his life again, a reunion with Maggie and his brothers, and a family of his own.

An arm looped through his, and Rex turned to see Tara beside him. How had she managed to escape?

"I have a surprise for you," she said. "Come on." She led Rex to where she'd parked a side by side. "Hop on."

Rex obliged, and they took off. It was like Tara's inner child was released, and by the time they arrived, Rex got down with shaky legs. He made a note to never allow Tara to drive him in a side by side again.

Then he realized they'd stopped in front of a familiar store.

Rex laughed. "Grandma Dee's?"

"Yes. Come on."

Rex hadn't been here since he got back, but the place appeared unchanged. He followed Tara until they reached the entrance.

Then Tara turned and faced him. "Hello, I'm Tara Rose." She extended her hand.

"And I'm Rex Oliver," Rex said as he shook her hand.

"Welcome to my store," she said with a smile.

"You bought it?" He'd heard Paul was retiring.

"Yes. Remember how Hailey's been talking about trying her hand at running a crafts store before heading off to college? She always said she wanted a good location that was special. And what better spot than the place where it all began for us? You know how much she loves the story of how we met, even though she pretends otherwise."

"You did great, honey. This is a great buy and prime real estate."

Tara beamed at his praise. "Besides, special news deserves to be shared in a special location."

Rex gave her a concerned look. "Is everything alright?"

Tara moved closer to him. "I'm pregnant, Rex, with our baby."

He was going to be a father again? "Are you serious?" She nodded. "Woohoo!" He threw his cowboy hat in the air. "Wait. Should you be walking outside in this cool air? Should I carry you?"

Tara laughed. "You're hilarious, you know that, right?"

Rex grinned. "I'm just madly in love with you."

"I love you, Rex Dexin."

"And I love you too, Tara Rose Ellis. Now let's go break the good news to our daughter. But no more side by sides or four-wheelers until we have this baby."

"Why?"

"We don't want her knocked out of your belly from the force of your driving."

Tara laughed again, the sound warming Rex's insides.

*Life is indeed good*, Rex thought as he kissed her.

Especially with the Doctor, who'd fallen in love with her Cowboy Enemy.

Jax watched the scene as everyone congratulated Rex and Tara on their engagement. It seemed his brother liked to do things backward—he'd gotten married first… or was it engagement, then marriage, and engagement again? It hurt his head just thinking about it.

But Jax was happy for his twin.

Even though they hadn't reconciled…

… and Jax found it hard to be in the same room with him.

Yet he was tired of traveling all the time, which he'd done to avoid Rex.

It wasn't that Jax didn't want things to be alright between them. Of course, he needed his brother back. But so much had happened between them, and Jax didn't know where to begin or how to fix their relationship.

And now Maggie was on his case to find a

woman he loved, since his brothers had all settled down.

But Jax wasn't interested in a relationship, had never been, even when Maggie had forced him to attend the singles mixer event.

Until he saw her.

The very opposite of what he'd ever imagined.

What was he going to do?

Thank you so much for reading! Want to know how Jax found love (in an enemies-to-lovers billionaire romance)?

Check out A DOCTOR BILLIONAIRE FOR THE COWBOY at https://dobidaniels.com.

Or want to know what happens next in Dexington? Sign up now at https://dobidaniels.com.

# ACKNOWLEDGMENTS

Writing a book is harder and more rewarding than I could have ever imagined. And it would not have been possible without the support, love, and encouragement from my number one cheerleader, my dearest mom. My life would never have been this awesome and wonderful without you.

Of course, I have to thank my precious little DC for his smiles and antics. You brighten my day and give me the strength to keep pushing through.

Thank you to my sisters for encouraging me on this wonderful journey. And a special thanks to my baby brother (who is so not a baby anymore) for being super supportive and checking in on my progress. You guys are the best.

Thank you to my wonderful author friends. You know who you are. Your selflessness and willingness to share what you know has made my writing journey smoother and an exciting one. And a special thanks to my ARC readers whose support have made a difference.

Most of all, I want to thank God who gave me life, surrounded me with the most wonderful people, and loved me all the way. You make my life complete.

And finally, a special thanks to all my readers whose love of my stories spur me on to write more. Thank you!

# ABOUT DOBI DANIELS

As a former physician and business executive in another life—with a childhood filled with reading multi-genre novels—Dobi Daniels loves to write sweet thrilling romance stories with heart. She enjoys dreaming up everyday characters who rise above unfavorable circumstances to overcome incredible odds and find joy along the way.

When not writing, Dobi can be found binging K-dramas and ice cream with her little sidekick by her side.

A Doctor Enemy for the Cowboy is the second book in A Cowboy Loves the Doctor Series. Sign up at dobidaniels.com to be notified when the next Dobi Daniels book comes out!

Thank you!

https://dobidaniels.com
hello@dobidaniels.com
facebook.com/dobidaniels
bookbub.com/profile/dobi-daniels
instagram.com/dobidaniels